Though there was ~~n~~ touching her, he
Deanna star~~...~~
her internal tempera~~ture~~...

And then he did something she didn't expect. He lowered his hand to her waist, then put his other hand on the other side of her waist.

Deanna didn't need the jacket to keep warm. Not at all…

"I never forgot about you," Eric said in a low, throaty voice.

Dusk had turned to dark since they'd arrived for dinner, and the streetlights provided the only illumination as they stood on the sidewalk. But Deanna wouldn't have needed that to see the heat swirling in Eric's eyes.

"I…" She didn't know what to say. This moment was surreal. Certainly one she'd never expected to experience. Not after she had run from Cleveland and left everyone and everything here in the rearview mirror.

"But truly," Eric went on, "*this* is what I thought about. Wondered about. Wished I'd gotten the chance to do."

"Hmm?" Deanna asked, not understanding.

But a moment later, Eric's comment became crystal clear when he placed a finger beneath her chin, tilted her head toward his, brought his mouth down onto hers and kissed her.

Books by Kayla Perrin

Kimani Romance

Island Fantasy
Freefall to Desire
Taste of Desire
Always in My Heart
Surrender My Heart
Heart to Heart

KAYLA PERRIN

has been writing since the age of thirteen and once entertained the idea of becoming a teacher. Instead, she has become a *USA TODAY* and *Essence* bestselling author of dozens of mainstream and romance novels and has been recognized for her talent, including twice winning Romance Writers of America's Top Ten Favorite Books of the Year Award. She has also won a Career Achievement Award for multicultural romance from *RT Book Reviews*. Kayla lives with her daughter in Ontario, Canada. Visit her at www.KaylaPerrin.com.

Heart
to
Heart

Kayla Perrin

KIMANI™
ROMANCE

Recycling programs
for this product may
not exist in your area.

ISBN-13: 978-0-373-86264-1

HEART TO HEART

For questions and comments about the quality of this book, please contact us at Customer_eCare@Harlequin.ca.

www.Harlequin.com

Printed in U.S.A.

Dear Reader,

If you've been reading my Harts in Love series, I hope you've thoroughly enjoyed Callie's and Natalie's stories. This is the final book in the trilogy, featuring the middle sister, Deanna.

Have you ever had a male best friend? He's the one you felt comfortable telling everything to, sharing all of your problems with. But…he's your friend. And though he has all of the qualities you want in a partner, you don't want to risk losing the friendship by taking a chance on love with him.

Sound familiar? Sometimes, we fear losing a friendship with someone who would otherwise be ideal for us. It's amazing how often we let fear stand in the way of what we want and need.

That's the dilemma Deanna faces. And just like those faced with this scenario in real life, she'll have to make a decision—cling to the friendship, or take a chance on love?

I hope you enjoy Deanna's journey!

Kayla Perrin

This book is dedicated to my parents' love story.
Forty-five years ago, they met each other and *knew*.

Sadly, my father's recent passing brought an end
to their forty-two-year marriage.

But one thing is certain:
Love never dies.

Cling to that, Mom.
Remember the love you shared.
In this world full of breakups and divorces,
you had something special and rare.
And it will never die.

Chapter 1

The woman's scream pierced the air. The room was dark, and she was struggling with the man, trying to escape his strong grasp. But the more she jerked and fought to free herself, the rougher he was with her.

She screamed again, a blood-curdling cry. And then the man slapped her. Slapped her so violently that she fell to the ground.

"Nooo!"

Deanna Hart awoke, bolting upright in the bed. Her chest was heaving, and her pulse was racing. And the sheets were damp with her sweat.

It took no more than a couple of seconds for her to realize that she'd been dreaming. That the last scream came not from the woman in her dreams but from her own lips.

Deanna drew in a deep breath, the image still fresh in her head. She'd had this dream before. And it was always the same. The man roughing up the woman. The woman being slapped and falling to the ground.

Every time, that's when Deanna woke up. As the woman fell to the floor in the dark room.

Her heart still beating rapidly, Deanna hugged her knees to her chest. She'd been having this dream ever since Brian James had hit her when she tried to end their relationship six months ago.

Glancing at the clock, she saw that it was just after three in the morning. The house was quiet and still. But she could hear the pounding of her heart in her ears.

Deanna was at her uncle Dave's house in Cleveland. She was out of harm's way. And yet, whenever she had this dream, she felt distinctly unsafe.

There are thousands of miles between you and Brian, she told herself as she lay back down and snuggled up against her pillows on the opposite side of the bed, where the sheets were still dry. *Besides, since that night, you haven't heard from him. There's no reason to fear him anymore.*

Her mental pep talk helped ease her mind. He had hit her only once, but it was a truly ugly exchange that Deanna never wanted to experience again in her life.

We're better off as friends, Brian. I realize that now.

You're breaking up with me?

We shouldn't have mixed business with pleasure. Things have become complicated. Let's finish my album first—

That was when Brian had violently grabbed and shaken her, and Deanna had been seized with fear. But she wasn't about letting a man terrorize her, so she had wriggled and pushed against him, struggling to get free of his grip.

"You think you're going to walk away from me?" Brian had screamed, spittle flying from his mouth. And as Deanna had continued to tussle with him, he had smacked her. Smacked her so hard that he'd busted her lip and drawn blood.

Seeing the blood, he had immediately looked horrified. Then he had apologized. Apologized over and over again, as if that would absolve him of what he'd done.

Deanna now understood how some people suffered post-traumatic stress for long periods of time over one life-altering event, because something about Brian's attack had left her with a disconcerting feeling. Even though she had cut off all contact with him, had not returned his calls and had not heard from him since April, here she was, away from Los Angeles for four months, and she was still dreaming about the attack.

Deanna frowned—there was something weird about the dream. Something she couldn't quite place. And it went beyond the fact that she couldn't see her own nor Brian's face. Every time she woke up, there was a sense of something that left her anxious. Because sometimes, she got the odd sensation that she wasn't even dreaming about her and Brian at all.

Which didn't make sense, of course. The nightmares had started only after Brian had assaulted her.

Deanna closed her eyes, but it took only a short time for her to realize that she wasn't going to fall back asleep. So she got out of bed, opened up her MacBook and did what she had done practically every day for the past three weeks. She went online to do a search for "Hart" in Georgia.

Georgia was a big state, and Deanna had been hoping to find a trace of her mother online. Ever since her sister Natalie had gone to Philadelphia to search for their mother and found a clue that pointed to her being in Georgia, Deanna had been extremely hopeful. Natalie had met a woman who had known their mother, and she had been adamant that Miriam Hart, who'd gone by a different name, had been in Philadelphia as recently as a few months earlier. According to this woman, Miriam had headed to Georgia to deal with an issue "once and for all."

What that issue was, Deanna had no clue. But during the

talks that she'd had with Natalie and their other sister, Callie, they'd come to the conclusion that something bad had happened with their mother and aunt. Auntie Jean had never talked about her parents, nor any other members of their extended family. As kids, neither Deanna nor her sisters had questioned that. Uncle Dave had had plenty of relatives, so they hadn't paid attention to the fact that Auntie Jean had none. Now, in the wake of their aunt's death—where no one from her side of the family had even shown up at the funeral—it finally dawned on them that something was odd.

Of course, Miriam and Jean's parents could have been deceased, and perhaps they had been the only two children. There were certainly logical explanations as to why Auntie Jean had never been in touch with extended family members.

She went back to deal with something once and for all....

Those were the words that gave Deanna pause. The words that had all of the sisters both hopeful and concerned.

Callie, the eldest sister and always the most rational in her thinking, was adamant that whatever their mother needed to deal with could have been taken care of in three months. Deanna tended to agree.

So where was she? Why hadn't she finally come back for them?

Was her mother still afraid of her old boyfriend, Rodney Cook, the man she had run from twenty-three years ago? Back then, Miriam had agreed to testify against him, but she had fled before doing so, deciding to take her chances on her own while leaving her three daughters with her sister. Did Miriam not know that Rodney was back behind bars? Could she still view him as a threat to her life all these years later?

Still so many questions, no answers.

Though Deanna had thus far not had success with her search, she would not be deterred. She opened her browser and typed in the White Pages search engine. It was easier to search city by city, so she chose one she hadn't already, looked up the Harts that were listed and saved those numbers in a document. Come morning, she would call each.

Callie's fiancé, Nigel, was, of course, doing things on his end as a police officer, and he certainly had more resources than Deanna and her sisters did. But Nigel's investigation had led to a dead end in Philadelphia. It was Natalie's search in the neighborhood that had yielded results.

Which only served to show that with more hard work and determination, Deanna and her sisters could track down their mother on their own if need be.

Finally exhausted, Deanna went back to bed, where she hoped she would sleep and not have another bad dream.

"Auntie Deanna," Kwame said excitedly. "Will you come to my school and talk to my class?"

Deanna looked up from her iPhone, where she had been once again searching for Harts in Georgia. Every one she had called that morning had led to more dead ends.

"What's that, sweetheart?" Deanna asked her nephew. She had zoned out of the family gathering at Callie and Nigel's place which was only a few blocks from Uncle Dave's. Having consumed a burger, potato salad and a cup of lemonade, Deanna had headed inside, where she had picked up her phone and begun her search again.

"Will you come to my school and talk to my new class?"

"Talk to your class?" Deanna repeated. "About what?"

"About your music!" Kwame said with enthusiasm. "You're famous. Everyone in my class is excited that you're my aunt. So I asked my teacher if you could come and talk to us, and she said that'd be awesome."

Deanna wouldn't exactly say that she was famous...not now, anyway. Not when she had dropped off the map for three years. But that wasn't something that Kwame needed to concern himself with. To him, she was an aunt who had had success in the music industry. There was no doubt that the kids in his class would be fascinated with her, as he was.

Kwame had asked her a million questions about her career, but the toughest one was, "When are you gonna make another album?"

That question had been the hardest to answer, and the most painful, given what had recently happened with Brian.

Pushing the thought from her mind, Deanna said, "Sure, hon. That sounds like something I can do."

"Cool!" Kwame exclaimed. Then he bounded out of the room and back onto the patio.

No sooner than he was gone Callie stuck her head through the door and said, "Why are you in here by yourself? Everyone's going to think that you're antisocial."

"Sorry," Deanna said. "I was just trying to check something." She held up her iPhone.

"That's the problem with today's technology—people are too addicted. They forget their families exist, even when they're at a family gathering."

"I know, I know," Deanna said. "And you're totally right. It's just…I was trying to find more leads regarding our mother. I keep feeling that the one clue we need is just around the corner."

"I hear you," Callie said. "And you know I want the same thing. But there'll be time for that later. Besides, who knows how many more beautiful weekends we'll have like this?"

Callie was right. It was mid-September, and the weather had already started to cool down. There had been some downright chilly days in the past couple of weeks, but today was bright and sunny, definitely a day that should be spent outside.

So Deanna slipped her phone into the pocket of her slacks and headed back out onto the patio. Happy chatter filled the air. It was a small gathering, the immediate family with one notable guest: Michael Jones.

Natalie was now dating the wide receiver for Cleveland, and they both seemed radiant. Even Uncle Dave's spirits had improved dramatically in the past month. Seeing two of his nieces find love was bringing him immeasurable joy.

Deanna's gaze went from Natalie and Michael, who were sitting side by side and holding hands, to Callie and Nigel. They both stood at the barbecue, where Nigel was placing the newly grilled corn onto a plate, and Callie was basting them with butter. The two had fallen into a happy, domestic routine, and to the outside world it would seem they had been together for years. Perhaps they had been—in their hearts. Deanna had never seen two people more in love than Nigel and Callie, and the fact that they had reunited after being apart for ten years proved that they had the kind of love that could stand the test of time.

"Grilled corn," Callie announced, walking with the plate toward the patio table. "Get it while it's hot."

"My favorite," Deanna said, snagging the first piece. The others quickly snatched up the remaining ones.

"So, Deanna," Callie said as she took a seat beside her. "Nigel's wondering if you have a boyfriend in California."

At the question, Deanna's eyes widened. "What?"

"A boyfriend," Callie repeated. "You know, someone you're seriously dating."

"I know what you mean." Deanna made a face. "But I'm wondering why the question. I've been here four months and you haven't heard me mention any male friend."

"I know," Callie said, "but Nigel didn't want to assume."

Deanna eyed her sister tentatively. "I don't have a boyfriend."

"Oh, good." Callie smiled. "So you're free and single."

Deanna noticed that Michael and Natalie were no longer

gazing into each other's eyes but staring at her with interest. She made a face. "I'm wondering why *Nigel* is concerned about the status of my love life."

Callie looked toward Nigel. He gave a nod, indicating his agreement for her to explain why. "Nigel has a friend at the police station," Callie said. "He thinks that maybe you two will hit it off."

Deanna raised both eyebrows. Her future brother-in-law was interested in her finding a man? Deanna highly doubted that. She would bet her last nickel that Callie had put him up to it, and maybe even Natalie, too. Now that both Callie and Natalie had found love, would they have a steady stream of police officers and football players for Deanna to choose from?

"So because both of my sisters are happily coupled off, I have to find someone, too?" Deanna asked.

"Something like that," Natalie said, grinning widely. Though she and Michael were sitting beside each other and holding hands, Natalie's legs were now extended and stretched out on Michael's lap. They were completely at ease together, totally content. Deanna didn't remember seeing her sister ever look quite so happy.

"And Nigel thinks that Marshall would love you," Callie went on. "You said he's a fan of her music, didn't you, sweetie?"

"Yep," Nigel agreed. "He said he's followed your career, loves your music, thinks you're beautiful."

Deanna refrained from rolling her eyes. She didn't want a man who liked her for her music. All too often, a man was enamored with her public persona and not the real her.

"If it's all well and good, I think I'll pass on being set up."

"Come on," Callie said. "What could it hurt?"

"I never do well on blind dates. I don't know why, I just

don't. I guess I feel too awkward, which causes the whole date to spiral downhill."

"Then don't think of it as a blind date," Callie said. "Think of it as an evening where you'll be meeting someone new."

"I'll still say no," Deanna said with a frown.

Callie shook her head. "So stubborn."

"What could it hurt to meet him?" Natalie asked. "Maybe Callie and Nigel could have us all over, so it'd be less awkward."

"Right now, the last thing on my mind is dating," Deanna said. "I'm more interested in finding our mother." She didn't want to add that the experience with her ex Brian had really shaken her. She could happily remain single for a long, long while.

Deanna hadn't chosen wisely before when it came to love. She'd had her heart broken, and she knew that she had also broken her share of hearts. There had been men who were into her—perfectly nice men whom she hadn't been able to give all of her heart. For the most part, her career had been her everything, her main focus.

Which was what made the demise of her relationship with Brian even harder to stomach. In a sense, he had been the perfect man for her because he was involved in the music industry. He was an established producer, and Deanna had met him at a party and had been ecstatic when he told her that he admired her music and wanted to work with her. It hadn't taken her long to realize that Brian was also romantically interested in her. They'd gotten along well, their banter had been easy and the flirtation had been fun. So Deanna had decided to throw caution to the wind and take a chance on love with Brian. She had begun to fantasize that they could become a music industry super-couple....

Instead, Deanna had learned a horrible lesson about mixing business with pleasure.

It was a lesson she had learned when she first left Cleveland and went to Hollywood. When, as a twenty-one-year-old girl, she met the man who would help get her career off the ground.

"Dee?" Natalie said tentatively.

Jerking her eyes to her sister's, and seeing the look of concern, Deanna realized that she was gripping the beer bottle in front of her...one that didn't even belong to her.

"You okay?" Natalie asked.

"Sure," Deanna replied, trying to sound as casual as possible.

She released the bottle, but she couldn't as easily release the painful memories that plagued her.

Chapter 2

Deanna saw Kwame waving enthusiastically as she approached the doors to his school. The same school she had attended as a child.

It was weird being here after all these years, like a definite step into the past. The building looked so much smaller than Deanna had remembered. Funny how when you became an adult your perspective changed.

It was two days after Kwame had asked if she would come talk to his class, and he had called her over the lunch hour to say that his teacher would like to meet her to discuss the idea. Deanna had promised that she would come at the end of the school day to speak with the teacher, which she guessed would be a meeting to determine how best to incorporate her visit with whatever studies the children were doing.

Kwame was beaming now as she approached, clearly thrilled at the fact that his idea of her talking to his class was one step closer to coming to fruition.

Deanna couldn't help but smile in return. A child's energy and happiness were infectious, and giving just a little bit of her time was clearly worth it. Just seeing how happy it made her nephew was already repaying her in leaps and bounds.

Kwame opened the door as she reached it, saying, "Auntie Deanna! I already talked to the principal about it, and he thinks it's a great idea. And he wants to meet you, too. Actually, he says he knows you already but that he wants to see you again."

Kwame was speaking in a rush, and Deanna quietly shushed him. "Whoa, you'll have to slow down. Your principal wants to meet me?"

"Uh-huh. He said he knows you."

"He knows me?" Deanna gave Kwame a skeptical look. "Or he knows who I am?" She would bet that it was the latter. Given that she had grown up in Cleveland, most people here knew that she was the Deanna Hart who had made a name for herself in the music industry.

"He knows you," Kwame stressed. He took her hand. "Come this way. He's in the office."

"I'm sure he means that he knows who I am," Deanna said as Kwame led her toward the office doors.

Kwame stopped mid-stride and faced her. "Uh-uh. He said he was excited about seeing you *again*."

"You mean he knows me knows me?"

"Yeah. He said he knew you before you got famous."

Deanna frowned slightly, now curious. Had she known any principals?

Before she even thought to ask the man's name, Kwame was opening the office doors and leading her inside. And that's when Deanna stopped dead in her tracks.

Eric Bell. Good Lord in heaven, was it really him?

His lips curled in a smile—the same room-brightening smile she had seen many times years ago—and Deanna was absolutely certain. Just over six feet tall, with that flawless golden-brown complexion—yep, it was definitely Eric Bell.

Her former boyfriend's brother.

"Eric?" Deanna said cautiously, though she knew it was him. He was more muscular than he had been before—most notably in his chest and his shoulders. And unlike years ago, he now had a neatly trimmed goatee framing his mouth. A decidedly sexier look, Deanna couldn't help thinking.

"Deanna." He stepped toward her, his dimples evident as he continued to grin. His smile always did exude warmth. It had brought her comfort in the aftermath of Marvin's betrayal. "You're back in town."

"I can't believe you're here." Though where she had expected him to be, she wasn't sure. "I can't believe you're the principal at this school."

"Is it really that surprising?" Eric asked. "I'd just started teaching when I knew you, and I used to say that I planned to become a principal one day."

She nodded, remembering now. But the truth was, she had forgotten about Eric's ambition. She had been so absorbed in her own drama at the time that his career goals hadn't been at the forefront of her mind. He had been her friend—the brother of the boyfriend who had done her wrong—and a person who had given her many pep talks and tried to help her get over Marvin. He had been a great support for her during her problems with Marvin and her sister Natalie—the sort of guy who could uplift anyone's spirits, and Deanna had known that he would be the kind of teacher kids would love.

"A teacher, yes," Deanna said. "I guess I didn't think you'd be a principal already. I mean, I thought a person would have to be a lot older to be a principal. I turned thirty this year, so that's got to make you, what, thirty-three, thirty-four?"

"Thirty-four in a few weeks. Good memory."

"But isn't that young to be a principal?" Deanna asked.

"Let's just say I dedicated myself to the pursuit of my career," Eric explained. "I was promoted to principal a year ago."

"Ah," Deanna said, nodding. That was something she could understand. Putting yourself completely into pursuing your passion—she had done the same.

She found herself glancing at his ring finger and noting that it was bare. Had he, like herself, lost out on relationship opportunities because he was so determined to succeed in his chosen field?

Why was she even wondering if he was married?

It was just that she wanted to know more about him. He had been her friend, and when she'd left town, she had dropped him like a hot potato. In part because her breakup with Marvin was such a hard experience for her at the time, and she hadn't wanted to relive those memories by staying in touch with Eric.

"I told you he knew you," Kwame said.

Deanna glanced down at her nephew. "Yes, you did."

"I think an old friend deserves a hug," Eric said.

When Deanna returned her gaze to him, she saw that he had opened his arms and was closing the distance between them. She walked into his embrace, noting as he enveloped her in a warm hug that he felt and smelled incredible.

Easing back, Eric said, "Why don't we go to my office?"

"Sure."

Both she and Eric turned at the sound of someone clearing their throat. Behind the counter in the office sat a biracial woman with long, tightly curled hair held back with a red headband.

"Oh, I'm sorry," Eric said. "Deanna, this is Michelle, the school secretary. Michelle, this is Deanna Hart."

"I know." Michelle beamed. "I'm a fan."

"Is that right?" Smiling, Deanna approached her and extended her hand. Michelle pumped it heartily. "Nice to meet you," Deanna added.

"The pleasure's all mine," Michelle told her.

Deanna glanced around the large office space. "This looks almost the same as it did twenty years ago," she commented. "Obviously it's had a paint job or two, and some of the furnishings are different, but other than that it hasn't really changed."

"The building's been updated in terms of repairs and fresh paint, but the idea was to keep it looking as much the way it did when it opened in 1955."

"And it does," Deanna said. "This is like a blast from the past."

Eric gestured to the open door about ten feet away. "My office is this way."

"A trip to the principal's office," Deanna said. "Should I be as concerned as the day I got in trouble for fighting Jenny Lawrence on the playground?"

Eric chuckled. "Not at all."

"You went to the principal's office when you were a kid?" Kwame asked, his tone saying he was surprised.

"A time or two," Deanna admitted sheepishly.

Kwame glanced at the wall clock. "Oh, I've got to head to my basketball practice."

"Sure thing," Deanna said. "I'll see you in a bit, then."

Kwame bounded out of the office—did the kid ever walk?—and Deanna followed Eric into the office, smiling softly as she saw his name on the gold plate on the door. PRINCIPAL E. BELL.

"Congrats on becoming principal," she told him, gazing around at the plaques on the wall. They highlighted his various educational accomplishments. "I'm very impressed."

"Thanks," Eric said. He closed the door. "Have a seat."

Deanna took a seat in front of his desk. Eric rounded the

desk and sank into his plush leather chair. Folding his hands in front of him, he merely stared at her for a few seconds. "It really is great to see you. I always wondered how you were doing."

"It's great to see you, too, Eric."

"I read about your aunt's death. I'm very sorry."

A wave of sadness washed over Deanna. "Thanks. It's been hard, but my aunt dying brought me and my sisters back to Cleveland. Which got us to work out our differences."

Eric nodded. "The proverbial silver lining. I know your aunt is looking down on you all with approval."

"Yes," Deanna agreed, a smile touching her lips. "I believe that, too."

"I sent you an email once," Eric said, changing the subject. "But you didn't respond."

"You did?"

"Yeah. To your website. I guess you get too many messages from fans to notice that one was from me. Either that or you didn't want to respond," he added, his tone lighthearted.

Deanna grimaced. "I'm sorry. Of course I would have responded had I seen your email. I didn't even check my messages—I had a couple of assistants do that for me. They shared some of the fan mail with me, but not all. They even sent out my responses. Sometimes they would flag certain messages and not respond if they thought they sounded suspicious. For example, if they thought someone was trying to use a feigned past association as a way to get to me, they especially wouldn't let me see the message."

Eric nodded. "Guess that's what happens when you become rich and famous."

"It all sounds so superficial, doesn't it?" Deanna commented. She had never been totally comfortable with letting others read and respond to her fan mail, but she'd been advised that it was the best way. "It was just easier to have someone else deal with the fan mail while I concentrated on the music."

"Of course. I wasn't passing judgment. Just letting you know that I tried to reach out to you."

"I'm the same girl you knew years ago," Deanna said. It was important that he know that. Yes, she had left and gone to Hollywood, but she had been running as much as she had been chasing a dream. Now that the dream had crashed and burned, she didn't even know if she wanted it anymore.

"I don't doubt that," Eric said. "It's why you're here right now. The fact that you're willing to talk to the students about what you do shows you're the type of person who wants to give back."

"It's no big deal," Deanna said, waving a dismissive hand.

"Don't sell yourself short," Eric said. "You talking to the students will be very inspiring. Your influence will be stronger than you know."

Deanna shrugged. "I certainly hope so."

"It will be, trust me. I've discussed your visit with Mrs. Mortensen, Kwame's teacher. And she said that any time you want to come in will be great."

"Oh," Deanna said. "I thought I was going to have a meeting with her this afternoon."

"Actually, I'm the one who wanted to speak to you."

"You?" Deanna asked. "To say hi?" she added with a soft chuckle.

"No. I wanted to speak to you because I have another idea in mind, as well. Something else for you to consider."

Deanna looked at Eric with a question in her eyes. "What's that?"

"Our eighth-grade drama club is going to be doing something different this year—a musical production. *Annie.* Peter Guy, our music teacher, was supposed to be directing the production. But he was recently in a bad car wreck and will be off for months. Sanjay Singh, one of our history teachers, stepped up to the plate to say he could take over directing."

"A history teacher?" Deanna questioned.

"He said he used to perform in community theater," Eric said with a shrug. "And he's helped Peter out with some plays in the past. Given the circumstances, I didn't have much choice. Yes, there's a new music teacher here in Peter's place, and I'm sure she could do an adequate job directing the musical production. But when Mrs. Mortensen talked to me about Kwame's suggestion, the idea came to me that I could ask you if you would mind helping out. Lend your musical expertise."

"You want me to work on your school's musical production?"

"In the capacity of a music coordinator, which really could be whatever you want it to be. The main thing would be to have you working with the children, which I hope might inspire some of them to come out of their shells."

"But I don't understand. If they're in a drama club, aren't they already outgoing?" All of the actor types Deanna knew in Hollywood were anything but shy.

"Not exactly," Eric said. "Some, yes. The drama club obviously attracts kids who are extroverts. But I've personally challenged some kids to join the drama club as a way to help boost their self-esteem. They're doing it because they respect me, and because I promised the group a trip to New York for an actual Broadway musical at the end of the year. They are capable of more than they believe they are, and they need a challenge—something they can conquer—that will help build up their self-image. I figured having someone like you here working with them might inspire them."

"That's a really great idea," Deanna said, not in the least surprised that Eric had become a principal at such a young age. He had a knack for figuring out ways to inspire people.

"Thanks. What do you think? The drama club meets twice

a week after school. Wednesdays and Thursdays. If you're interested, you could come tomorrow."

"'I'd be happy to help out," Deanna said.

"Now, it would be a volunteer position—"

"Oh, that's fine," Deanna interjected. "I don't need to be paid to help out with a school production." She still had a healthy bank account, and giving back was one of the things that she wanted to do in a more meaningful way. It was one thing to donate cash to causes but another thing altogether to actually work at something where you made a difference. She had seen how much joy Natalie had gotten from working with the Compassion For Families charity, how gratifying that had been for her.

"Yeah?" Eric asked. "It'll be a good couple months of work. Once a week in the beginning, but likely a few times a week as the production date gets near."

"Which is perfectly fine with me." She paused. "Though I have to be honest. There are a few things going on in my life that might demand my time unexpectedly. I anticipate being available for every rehearsal, but something might come up. As long as that won't be a problem…"

"It's a volunteer position," Eric said, and he gave her a look as if to say he couldn't expect her to give up her life for the cause. "That's not a problem…unless you realize you can't make it to most of the rehearsals."

"I'm in town for the foreseeable future." She was certainly in no rush to get back to Hollywood.

"Great. When you come tomorrow, I'll introduce you to Mr. Singh."

"I look forward to it." A beat passed, then Deanna pushed her chair back and said, "All right. Tomorrow, then."

"Actually," Eric began. "What are you doing right now?"

"Now?" Deanna repeated. "I was just going to head back

home. Though since I'm here, I figured I'd watch Kwame at his basketball practice, then drop him home."

"So, no plans for the evening?" Eric pressed on.

"Nothing in particular, no."

"Then perhaps I can persuade you to join me for dinner after you've dropped Kwame off?" Eric smiled, a warm and charming smile that brightened his whole demeanor. "I was going to head to a restaurant for dinner tonight—something I'd much prefer to do with company."

"You're inviting me out to dinner?" Deanna asked in a playful tone.

"Why not? We can catch up on old times."

"Nearly nine years," Deanna commented wistfully. "A lot has happened for both of us since then."

"That's for sure, superstar."

"Oh, stop," Deanna told him.

"Seriously, though. I want to hear about everything. How you made your career happen. Everything."

And then there was something about the way Eric's gaze held hers that made her think that "everything" included hearing about her love life.

Or was it just Deanna who was interested in his? Because when she'd looked around his office, she hadn't seen pictures of him and a special female. Which surprised her, given that Eric was certainly an eligible bachelor. He was gorgeous, amiable, inspiring and easy to talk to. And he didn't have a phone full of female contacts he could call to join him for dinner? How come a woman hadn't already swept him off his feet?

"So, what do you say?" Eric asked. "Are you going to leave me to eat dinner by myself?"

It had been eight years since she had seen Eric, almost nine. And she had always enjoyed their conversations. His friendship was one she'd cherished, one she shouldn't have let slide when she left town.

"Dinner with an old friend?" Deanna began. "How can I say no to that?"

Dinner with an old friend.

Eric felt an odd sensation in his stomach at her words. He had been an old friend…and yet he felt the term didn't adequately sum up the nature of their past relationship.

All those times he had held Deanna as she had cried. Held her and treasured the feeling of her in his arms.

Held her and hoped…

Marvin, Marvin. Deanna had been so obsessed with his lying, cheating brother that she hadn't been able to see a life beyond him. Eric had tried, as gently as he could, to tell her that she could do a heck of a lot better than Marvin, if only she would open her eyes.

Well, she'd opened them all right. Opened them and run clear to California.

He had hoped that she would—

Eric promptly cut the thought off. Why was he letting himself get distracted by thoughts of the past? The only thing that mattered right now was that he was truly happy to see Deanna. He had missed her all of these years. She'd left and cut her ties to Marvin, as well as to him. He'd been able to know she was alive and relatively how she had been doing by following her career in the media. There hadn't been news of her dating this actor or that musician, which he'd always been happy about, though he suspected that she'd simply kept her love life out of the news.

His eyes took in her features now. Nine years had aged her face in only the most positive ways. She looked more mature, more womanly. And even more striking than she had when he had last seen her in person. Some stars were always touched up when they were in photos and on television to the point where they almost looked like different people without makeup. But Deanna's caramel skin was blemish-free, and with only minimal makeup on, she was a knockout. Her beautiful smile exposed a set of perfect, white teeth, and her long lashes framed wide, expressive eyes. The kind of eyes that seemed to reach right through the screen and touch a person's soul. It had been no surprise to Eric that she had done well in the music industry. She had the look of a star.

"Why are you looking at me like that?" Deanna asked, glancing away uncomfortably.

"Your hair," Eric quickly said, clearing his throat. "It's shorter than it used to be."

Deanna fingered the short hair at her nape. "You like it?"

"Yes, it's very nice," he replied.

She offered him a small smile. "So, as for dinner, did you have a particular place in mind?"

"Yeah, I did. Unless there's a particular place you want to go."

"I wouldn't mind going to A Taste of Soul," Deanna told him.

"Ah, Michael Jones's restaurant," Eric said.

"Yeah. The food is great. Have you been?"

"A few times."

"And you like it?"

"It's a great restaurant. Let's go."

"Good. Here's some news. Michael Jones and my sister are dating."

"Really?" Eric asked, surprised. "Natalie?"

"Yeah. I don't know if you heard on the news about her divorce from Vance Cooper, the one who plays for the NBA?"

Eric nodded. "Definitely. I was sorry to hear about it. So many of these men out there get a good woman and don't know what to do with her."

Deanna nodded, looking at him with a curious expression in her eyes. Eric wondered what she was thinking, but she didn't say.

"Anyway," Deanna continued, "I've been there once, and the food is fantastic. Whether my sister was dating Michael or not, I'd go there again."

"Of course. The food is great, the atmosphere is lively. What's not to like?"

Finally, Deanna stood. Eric did as well. "I'll drop Kwame home, then get ready. When should I meet you there? Is six o'clock good?"

"Sure. That's great."

Eric spoke casually, but he was all too aware of the familiar flush spreading over his body. The one he'd had every time he had held her close in the past, and when he'd watched her on TV.

He had waited nearly nine years for this moment, this opportunity to see Deanna without the shadow of his brother hanging over their heads.

And in just over two hours, he was going to make the most of it.

Chapter 3

Though Deanna had been more than appropriately dressed for dinner—wearing boot-cut jeans, a white blouse and a black velvet blazer—she went back to Uncle Dave's place and changed. Her outfit now was decidedly more upscale. She was used to dressing up and going out to fancy dinners in L.A., and she relished the opportunity to put something on now that was a little fancy.

Though, as she looked at her reflection in the mirror, she couldn't help wondering if she had gone a little overboard.

She was wearing a black sheath dress and low-heeled black sling-backs encrusted with colorful jewels. Her hair was short, so she didn't have to worry about fussing over that. She slicked it back, added some mousse so it would stay in place and concentrated on the features that she liked to accentuate. She added mascara to her lashes, eyeliner and a burgundy shade of lipstick.

Uncle Dave's wide eyes and low whistle when she came

downstairs made it clear she had dressed to impress. "You going to some fancy award show?" he asked her.

Deanna chuckled as she went over to him where he sat on his recliner, then gave him a kiss on the forehead. "No. I ran into an old friend. He's taking me out for dinner."

"Hmm…another romance brewing?"

"He's an old friend," Deanna stressed. "You remember the guy Natalie and I were fighting over all those years ago?"

Uncle Dave frowned. "Tell me you're not going out with Marvin!"

"No. Definitely not. His brother, Eric, is the principal at Kwame's school. I saw him today. And we're going out now to catch up on old times."

"Hmm." Uncle Dave gave her a curious look. "Dressed like that?"

"I've got a suitcase full of nice clothes I haven't had a chance to wear," Deanna told him. Then she started for the door. "See you in a couple of hours."

A short while later, when Deanna got out of her car and walked toward Eric where he stood waiting outside of the restaurant, the first thing she noticed was the way his eyes widened as he took in her appearance.

"You changed," he said, his voice laden with approval.

"I figured I may as well get dressed up for the occasion. It's not every day you run into an old friend and get the opportunity to get reacquainted."

Deanna wasn't sure if Eric even heard her reply, because his eyes drank in her appearance from head to toe, as though he was transfixed. "Wow. Seriously, wow. You are ravishing."

For some reason, Deanna felt a tingling sensation in her belly. "Thank you."

Eric made a sweeping hand gesture, indicating his outfit and frowning slightly. "I didn't get to change."

"You look great," she told him. And he did. His black

slacks, beige shirt and black blazer looked good on him. He had taken off the tie he'd been wearing at school earlier, which now made his professional look more GQ sexy.

"All the same, I wish I'd been able to vamp it up a notch to truly complement you."

"Now you're making me wish I hadn't changed," Deanna said.

"Nonsense," Eric told her. "I'm glad you went to the effort to get dressed up for me."

"I'm glad you approve."

His eyebrows wriggled as he offered her his elbow, and Deanna cocked her head as she slipped her arm through his.

What were they doing? Flirting?

The question fled her mind as Eric opened the door and led them into A Taste of Soul. They were immediately greeted with a bright smile from a pretty young woman behind the hostess stand.

"Table for two?" the woman asked.

"Yes," Eric and Deanna said at the same time.

The woman picked up two menus and then began to lead them into the restaurant. Eric commented, "I wonder if we'll see Michael Jones."

"The owner, Michael Jones?" the hostess asked, looking over her shoulder at them. "He's not here."

"He's headed out of town for an away game," Deanna explained. "My sister went with him."

The hostess stopped at a four-top table near the window and set the menus down on it. Then she placed her hands on her hips as she looked at Deanna. "Your sister's— Of course, you're Deanna Hart."

"That's me."

"I'm Sandra." She extended her hand, and Deanna shook it. "Nice to meet you."

"Nice to meet you as well, Sandra. This is Eric, a friend of mine."

"I've never seen Michael so smitten," Sandra commented. "He's really into your sister."

"That's good to hear, because she's really into him."

"Vivian will be your server tonight," Sandra told them. "She'll be out shortly."

"Sounds like it's going really well between your sister and Michael Jones," Eric commented once Sandra walked away. He pulled Deanna's chair out for her.

"It is," Deanna said, sitting. "It's almost like they were destined to meet." Eric helped push her chair back under the table, and Deanna grinned up at him. "Why, thank you. You are certainly a gentleman."

Eric sat opposite her. And even though Deanna had lifted the menu and was perusing it, she could sense his eyes on her.

"What?" she asked, looking at him and finding that, yes, he was staring. She touched her hair self-consciously.

"Just thinking about how odd it is that we're both here, about to have dinner. Given that I thought I'd never see or talk to you again."

"I know. When I woke up this morning, I never dreamed I'd be here with you this evening." Deanna paused. "Sometimes life offers you nice surprises."

"You remember all those talks we used to have?" Eric asked.

"Are you kidding?" Now Deanna made a slight groaning sound. "But most of them, I would rather forget."

"Why?"

"Why?" Deanna repeated, bulging her eyes. "The way I cried over Marvin like a fool? What you must have thought of me."

"I thought you were a beautiful woman who'd fallen for the wrong man. It happens. A lot."

Deanna shrugged and again looked at the menu. But she knew what she was going to have. The last time she'd been here, she had contemplated the Cajun catfish with collard greens but passed it over for the gumbo. "I'm having the catfish," she announced.

"That's a great choice," Eric said. "I'm going to have the same." He closed his menu. "You want wine?"

"White?" Deanna asked.

"White's good. Sauvignon blanc?"

"Excellent choice."

Vivian, the waitress, arrived with a basket of warm corn bread, which Deanna dug into as Eric placed their orders. She then promised to be back with the wine momentarily.

Deanna looked toward the stage area, where an attractive young man had just appeared. He looked stylish in a fedora, cream-colored dress shirt with tie, dark jeans and black loafers. A few people cheered as he sat behind the keyboard, which led Deanna to believe that they were already acquainted with this musician.

"So, what have you been up to for the past nine years?" Deanna asked.

"Other than dedicating myself to work?"

"Certainly it couldn't have been all work, no play," Deanna said. "You're not wearing a wedding ring, but that doesn't mean you're not married."

"Why?" Eric asked, giving her a playful look. "You interested?"

"Just wondering," Deanna said. "A lot can happen in nine years."

The musician hit a few keys on the keyboard and then paused. "Evening, ladies and gentlemen. My name is Trey Martinez."

There were more hoots and whistles. Then Trey began to

play. Moments later, he began to sing. He had a sultry, smooth sound and reminded her of Brian McKnight.

Deanna turned back to Eric. "So?" she prompted. "Are you going to answer my question?"

Eric swallowed the piece of corn bread he'd bitten before answering. "Actually, I was married. But it didn't last long. Not quite two years."

Deanna looked at him, into his handsome face and bright eyes. Maybe it was the love ballad that Trey was singing, and the romantic atmosphere with two lit candles on the table. But it struck her just how totally sexy Eric was. She hadn't truly taken notice of this fact years ago, because she'd been so obsessed with Marvin. But there was no denying it now.

Eric was superfine.

Which prompted the question, why would any woman let him go?

"Why did you divorce?" Deanna couldn't help asking.

And that was when she saw the first sign of discomfort flash in Eric's eyes. So much so that she quickly said, "You don't have to tell me. It's really none of my business."

"We just…we just didn't see eye to eye on everything. Irreconcilable differences, if you will."

Vivian returned with the two glasses of wine. With an amiable smile, she placed them on the table and then went on her way. She seemed to be the type of server who believed in being unobtrusive, and Deanna appreciated that.

"I made mistakes," Eric went on, still talking about his marriage. "I was focused on my career. I'm not saying I ignored my wife, but she wanted me to take her out to dinners all the time, to the movies, the theater. And we did go out— don't get the wrong idea. But not all the time the way she wanted. And one other thing she really hoped for that I hadn't realized when we got married was that I would travel with her during the summer. She had dreams of going to Italy with me, to a cooking school in Tuscany for a few weeks—which I wasn't opposed to, but the summer after we married was out of the question. I was working on completing my second master's, and she wasn't happy that I wouldn't go with her." Eric sighed softly. "I knew that I wanted to achieve certain goals by a certain time. I was focused on that. So focused that I didn't realize I was losing my wife."

He had recited these facts so casually that Deanna had to wonder if he had been at all heartbroken over the downfall of his marriage.

"You didn't even make the two-year mark?" she asked.

"One year, nine months. Ellie said it wasn't working, that we weren't on the same page. And I agreed."

Deanna sensed that there was more to the story, something important that he was leaving out. Or was it just that in her experience, things weren't so black and white? "You seem so…I don't know—comfortable about everything?" she said to him. "I'm sure it must have been a terrible time for you."

"Ellie is a great girl, and I wish her nothing but happiness and success. But we weren't right for each other. We were two friends who both wanted to get married and thought, hey, why not to each other? But we weren't meant to be."

"You say that so matter-of-factly."

"We're still friends. Ellie has gone on to marry someone else. Now she's the wife of some cruise ship director, and I understand that they travel quite a bit. She's happy. And I'm happy for her."

"I see," Deanna said. Maybe she was reading into things, thinking there was more to the story than there really was. "Well, it happens."

"And sometimes things happen for a reason." Eric held her gaze as he raised his wineglass. "To new beginnings."

And as Deanna looked into Eric's magnetic eyes, she was

struck once again with just how gorgeous he was. She clinked her glass against his. "To new beginnings."

The patrons applauded as Trey finished his first song, and he promptly began the second one. "What about you?" Eric asked. "I've never heard any reports that you were married, but that doesn't mean you never tied the knot."

Deanna shook her head. "No. I never got married." She paused. "Perhaps I was a little like you. Very focused on my career."

"I bought your albums," Eric said. "And I'm not saying this just because I know you, but you're supremely talented."

"Thank you," Deanna told him.

"You have anything new coming out?" Eric asked. "I've been waiting for the next album to drop."

Deanna deliberately lifted her wineglass to her mouth and took a sip. Eric watched her every movement. She felt as though a spotlight were on her as she swallowed, then finally spoke. "Well, not right now," she answered, hoping he didn't pick up on the discomfort in her tone. "I was working on some stuff, but…not anymore."

Eric gave her an odd look, but he didn't press her for details. Maybe it was obvious to him that she didn't want to talk about it, and for that she was glad. She didn't want to get into the story about Brian.

"I'm surprised you haven't asked me about Marvin." Eric chuckled softly.

Deanna rolled her eyes in a playful manner. "I think it's fair to say I did more than enough talking about him nine years ago. I can't believe how pathetic I was."

"You weren't pathetic. You were…passionate."

Deanna's eyebrows shot up. "Passionate?"

"Yeah. You used to be so full of fire whenever you spoke to me about Marvin. You got so heated when you complained about him doing you wrong."

Deanna cringed as she remembered just how often she had complained about Marvin. Had she been smart, she would have dumped him without a second thought the moment she had learned about him and her sister and not looked backward. Instead, she had fought for him—and helped ruin her relationship with Natalie in the process. "Ugh...so young and stupid."

"Not young and stupid. Young and hopeful was more like it."

"You always were good at putting a positive spin on everything." Deanna sighed. "I guess I may as well ask—what happened to Marvin? What's he doing with his life?"

"My brother." Eric rolled his eyes. "Same old Marvin. You talked about being young and foolish—well, he's now older and still foolish. I hoped he would grow out of his player ways, but he didn't. He's on a second divorce now."

"What?"

Eric nodded. "Yep. He was married to a girl from here, really nice girl he met in college, Beverly."

"I remember Beverly. Beverly Bonaparte?"

"Yeah, that's her."

"I can't say that I'm surprised." Deanna shook her head. "Wow." Then she said, "Okay, I'm over it. What happened to their marriage?"

"What you'd expect of Marvin. Beverly loved him, but, yup, he cheated on her. Time and again. They have two kids, twins. A boy and a girl. The so-called perfect family. But not for Marvin. Nope, he wasn't happy unless he could have more women. Sometimes I wonder how it's possible that we're related."

"I wondered the same thing many times myself."

Something changed in Eric's expression. Giving her a pointed look, he asked, "Is that all you wondered?"

Butterflies fluttered in Deanna's belly. Suddenly, she didn't know what to say.

Eric held her gaze for a moment longer, then smiled softly and reached for more corn bread. "Anyway," he went on, "Beverly and Marvin divorced, then Marvin headed to New Orleans to be with some other woman. Beverly moved to Cincinnati, so we hardly see the kids."

"Oh, that's awful," Deanna said. But she was all too aware that Eric had just let her off the hook concerning whatever he had been curious about.

"Tell me about it. The twins are five, and I try to stay in touch with Beverly as much as possible. But she's remarried, so she doesn't have as much time for us as she used to. I think in the beginning she stayed away a lot because she didn't like the reminders of Marvin. And because things had gotten ugly between them. Sometimes, the extended family can't help but become casualties when divorce happens."

Deanna nodded. She was thinking about Callie. Callie and Nigel hadn't divorced, but she hadn't been able to know her nephew until now because Callie had left, fearing that any contact with any of them would've led to Nigel finding out that she'd had his child. Thank goodness, they had all reunited—and now Callie and Nigel were together the way they should have been in the beginning.

Deanna shared that story with Eric, and when she was finished he said, "You would never know they'd been apart. Kwame talks about his mother and his father as though they were always together. He seems well-adjusted and happy."

A smile touched Deanna's lips. "He is. He's elated to have met his father and thrilled that his parents are back together. You'd never know that he hadn't been in Nigel's life until a few months ago."

Vivian arrived at the table with their dinner orders. "Two Cajun catfish dinners," she announced, placing the steaming plates on the table in front of them. "Now, if you need anything else, let me know."

"Sure thing," Eric told her.

"It smells delicious," Deanna commented.

"Wait till you taste it."

Deanna did exactly that and then moaned in pleasure. "Oh, wow. This is amazing."

Eric cut a morsel of his fish but held it in front of his mouth as he spoke again. "It sounds like your sister and Nigel had issues to work out, and as hard as it must have been for you all, having to come back here for your aunt's funeral allowed healing to take place."

"You're right about that," she said, but she couldn't help thinking that Eric was truly insightful. Perhaps that was why she had been compelled to tell him her problems as a teenager. He was the kind of guy who got it.

"Sadly, Marvin is hardly in his kids' lives. I don't think he sees them at all."

"It's tragic, isn't it? People divorce, and suddenly they're not a part of their children's lives. It shouldn't be that way." Deanna paused. "You said Marvin is on divorce number two?"

"Yep. He was married to this other girl for two years. No surprise, she left him. And the worst part is, she has a child with him, too. I've only seen his daughter once."

"Wow."

"I hardly talk to my brother," Eric admitted. "He's shacked up with some other woman in Louisiana. I don't think he'll ever get it."

Silence fell between them, and they began to eat their dinners while listening to the smooth sounds of Trey Martinez. The man was good.

Deanna was halfway through her meal when she felt Eric's eyes on her. Slowly, she lifted her gaze and saw that yes, he was looking at her.

And something about the way he was staring at her made her breath catch in her throat.

"How old is your other niece?" she asked, hoping to alleviate the awkward tension she was now feeling.

"Cecelia's eighteen months old," Eric said.

No, it wasn't awkward tension, Deanna realized. She was very distinctly feeling a sexual rush. But she tried to ignore it. "And what are the twins' names?"

"Devon and Daneesha."

"I bet they're darling."

"They are," Eric confirmed. A beat passed, then, "You know what I'd really like to talk about?"

Deanna shook her head slightly, but her stomach was still fluttering.

"No," she told him.

"I'd like to talk about us." Eric held her gaze, his eyes not wavering. "About you and me."

Chapter 4

For some reason, Deanna felt a wave of heat envelop her. You and me.

What exactly did he mean by that?

"Us?" she asked faintly, wondering why her pulse had picked up speed.

"All those years ago, when you used to come to me and cry on my shoulder about Marvin, did you never…" His voice trailed off.

"Did I never what?" Deanna asked.

Eric paused, and Deanna wondered if he wasn't going to finish his statement. And she wanted him to, wanted to hear what he had to say.

"Did you never wonder about me? Did you never look at me in the way that you looked at Marvin?"

She felt a tightening in her chest, the kind she felt when she was attracted to someone. And yet, there was only one way to answer the question honestly. "I was so wrapped up in Marvin that someone else could have come into my life with a neon sign from God shining on him that said he was Mr. Right, and I wouldn't have noticed."

Eric grinned, and not for the first time Deanna noticed the way the faint lines around his eyes crinkled when he smiled, as well as those two little dimples in his cheeks. Had he always been this good-looking?

"I like that," he told her. "What you said. It set up a really great visual image."

Deanna shrugged. "The songwriter in me, I guess."

"What about now?" Eric asked.

Deanna looked away for a moment, then back at him. "Now…" She drew in a deep breath. "There's no denying that you're an attractive man," she said, "but we've always been friends."

"And you don't want to cross the friendship line?" Eric said, point blank.

"I…this is all out of left field," Deanna admitted.

"For you, maybe. I was always interested in getting to know you better, but you only had eyes for my brother."

"What?" Deanna gave him a questioning look. "Are you serious?"

"Yeah," Eric said softly. "But you were my brother's girl. And even if you weren't, I was nearly four years older than you, which is ancient when you're nineteen. I knew that you never looked at me that way. Why am I even telling you this?"

Deanna shifted in her seat. This was getting somewhat uncomfortable. She liked Eric, and he seemed to be the same decent guy he always was. Not to mention that he was easy on the eyes. But…

"I haven't seen you in almost nine years," Deanna said.

"And I never forgot you in all that time. I guess what I'm saying is that I hope that now—without Marvin or anyone else between us—maybe you and I can get to know each other on a different level."

He was serious. Deanna had to take a moment to digest everything Eric had just confessed to her.

"This guy's good," Eric commented, indicating Trey Martinez at his piano.

"Yeah," Deanna agreed. "Really talented."

"You going to have dessert?" Eric asked.

"I wasn't planning on it," she told him.

"The peach crumble is great. Maybe we can share it."

"Okay, you've twisted my arm. Let's get one each."

Eric raised a hand to flag down Vivian, and she came over to the table. "Two peach crumbles," he told her.

"How was the catfish?" Vivian asked.

"Fantastic," Deanna told her.

"Great." Vivian collected their plates. "Any coffee?"

"I'll have one," Eric said.

"Me, too," Deanna chimed in.

And as Vivian sauntered away, Deanna couldn't help thinking about Eric's bombshell. Was it true? Had he always been interested in her?

And how did she feel about that?

Just the question caused her stomach to tingle. There was no doubt that she was feeling a definite attraction to him today. For the first time, she was seeing him for what he was—a man, and not just a sounding board. What wasn't there to like? He was tall, handsome, well-spoken. It wasn't like pulling teeth to get information from him. He was the kind of guy who knew how to talk to a woman. That was hugely appealing.

But he was also her friend. And Deanna was no good at relationships. She had proven that time and again.

She'd had girlfriends who'd dated their male buddies, only for it to end in disaster. And then not only was the relationship over, but the friendship was, as well. Deanna could easily explore more with Eric…but at what cost?

The desserts came, which they ate while enjoying Trey's music. He finished a particularly poignant song about love and loss to huge applause, after which he bowed and thanked everyone for listening. "I've got CDs for sale," he added. "Only ten dollars. If you're interested, come on up."

Lifting her clutch purse off of the table, Deanna stood. "Ten dollars is a steal. I'm going to get one."

She noticed others were approaching Trey, also eager to buy his CD. As she waited, she pulled two twenties out of her wallet. And when it was her turn to step up to Trey, she said, "I'll take two."

He began to scrawl his signature on the first case with a silver Sharpie. "You enjoyed the show?"

"Oh, no doubt," Deanna told him. "You were amazing." As a musician, she knew how nice it was to receive feedback. "Definitely very talented."

"Thanks," he said, beaming. "That means a lot, coming from someone like you."

"Someone like me?"

He gave her a knowing look. "I know who you are," he said. "And yeah, to hear that you enjoyed my music just made my night."

He passed her the signed CDs, and she saw that on the top one he had written *Ms. Hart, it's a pleasure!!* Which only confirmed that he knew exactly who she was.

"Thank you," Deanna told him. Then she gave him the money.

"No problem," Trey said, accepting the bills and heartily shaking her hand. Then he noticed that she'd given him two twenties and said, "You gave me too much."

He offered her back a twenty, but Deanna waved a dismissive hand. "That's a steal for the entertainment you provided."

And she was suddenly struck with an idea. For the past few years, she thought that to continue her career meant releasing another album. But that wasn't necessarily true. She could just as easily have a fulfilling career singing at small venues and clubs. Performing in a more intimate setting, like she had at the charity auction her sister had hosted last month.

"Hopefully I'll see you here again," she told Trey.

"Every Tuesday night, six-thirty."

Deanna felt the hand creep around her waist then, and tingles of pleasure shot through her side. She looked to her right, into Eric's handsome face. And her heart began to thud hard. Good Lord, Eric's hand felt good on her body.

His fingers splayed over her hip, and a slow breath oozed out of Deanna. She missed a man touching her like this, she realized.

Eric offered his free hand to Trey. "Great show."

Trey pumped his hand. "Thanks, man."

"I've settled the bill," Eric told her as he led her a few steps away.

"Oh, thank you." She passed him one of Trey's CDs. "And this is for you."

Eric eyed the CD. "Great, thanks."

His hand stayed on her waist as he led her to the restaurant's exit. Deanna felt warring emotions inside of her. On one hand, she wanted to throw caution to the wind and tell Eric that she wanted to go back to his place with him. She was certain that he would be an excellent lover.

But on the other hand, she couldn't stop thinking about the fact that this was Eric, Marvin's older brother. A friend she had always been able to count on.

A friend she didn't want to lose again.

They said goodbye to the hostess and then headed to the door. Eric released her as he pushed the door open and held it for Deanna to pass.

Deanna felt a little chill as she stepped outside and the night air enveloped her, and she rubbed her arms.

"Here." Eric slipped off his blazer and put it around Deanna's shoulders.

"Thanks," she said.

"I bet you forgot how cool it can get here, living in sunny California."

"California has its share of cold days," Deanna told him. "I really enjoyed the dinner. It was nice to get out," she added.

"No problem. Thank you for joining me."

She began to shrug out of his jacket. "I'll be fine getting to my car. It's just around the corner."

Eric placed a hand on her shoulder, stopping her from removing the jacket. "You can return it tomorrow."

"Oh. Okay."

Though there was no need for him to continue touching her, he didn't remove his hand. Deanna stared up at him, feeling her internal temperature rise.

And then he did something she didn't expect. He lowered his hand to her waist, then put his other hand on the other side of her waist.

Deanna didn't need the jacket to keep warm. Not at all…

"I never forgot about you," Eric said in a low, throaty voice.

Dusk had turned to dark since they'd arrived for dinner, and the streetlights provided the only illumination as they stood on the sidewalk. But Deanna wouldn't have needed that to see the heat swirling in Eric's eyes.

"I…" She didn't know what to say. This moment was surreal. Certainly one she'd never expected to experience. Not after she had run from Cleveland and left everyone and everything here in the rearview mirror.

"But truly," Eric went on, "this is what I thought about. Wondered about. Wished I'd gotten the chance to do."

"Hmm?" Deanna asked, not understanding.

But a moment later, Eric's comment became crystal clear when he placed a finger beneath her chin, tilted her head upward to his, brought his mouth down onto hers and kissed her.

He kissed me.

It was all Deanna could think about later as she lay in bed, wondering what exactly had happened.

One minute, she had been going out for dinner with an old friend to catch up on all that had happened in his life over the years. The next, he had been revealing that he'd always been attracted to her.

And then he had laid one on her.

Deanna felt warmth as she thought about it. Her toes actually wiggled. Oh, boy—did Eric ever know how to kiss a woman....

Right there on the sidewalk, as his mouth had come down on hers, she was lost. His velvety smooth lips had made the sweetest contact with hers, and Deanna had sighed with pleasure.

The kiss had been full of fire, eliciting passion while respectfully not crossing the line. He had left her bedazzled while kissing her without using his tongue. Instead, his lips had skillfully and teasingly played over hers. And when he had softly suckled her bottom lip, Deanna had thought she would go mad with lust.

That's what she was feeling now as she lay on her bed. Lust.

It had been a long time since she had slept with a man. She and Brian had gone to bed only a few times, and she hadn't felt a smidgen of the fire and passion in his bed as she had tonight while kissing Eric on the street.

Before Brian, it had been a good year since her last relationship. And she hadn't really missed the sex.

But now...

Deanna rolled onto her back and closed her eyes. Closed her eyes and replayed the kiss with Eric in her mind.

They hadn't even exchanged phone numbers—she was going to see him tomorrow, anyway—but she was so hot and bothered that a part of her wished she could call him now, that she could pay him a visit....

"What am I thinking?" she asked herself. "One decent kiss and you're thinking about getting naked? Deanna, what is wrong with you?"

Though in all fairness, it had been more than a decent kiss. It had been an amazing kiss.

So amazing that she couldn't wait for the hours to pass so that she could see him again at school tomorrow.

No doubt about it, the kiss had been worth the wait.

Eight years and ten months after the last time he had seen her, Eric had finally done what he'd always wanted to do. Tasted Deanna's lips to see if they were as sweet as he imagined they would be.

And, man, were they ever! He had heard people say that a kiss could determine if there were truly sparks between people, and based on the kiss he and Deanna had shared, they had generated enough heat to melt the snow in Cleveland on a winter's day.

He'd heard her soft purr of protest when he broke the kiss. Had seen the dazed look in her eyes as he gazed down at her.

Yes, the kiss had come out of the blue—at least for her. But it had proven a point.

They had chemistry.

The kind of chemistry Eric couldn't wait to experience in a bedroom.

But that wasn't all that he wanted, which was why he knew better than to push things too quickly. As much as he suspected—based on the fact that after the kiss Deanna had asked him if he was just heading home—that another kiss or two and she would have been agreeable to spending the night with him, he had refrained.

Because the chemistry certainly wasn't one-sided, and they were bound to explore their sexual connection sooner or later.

In the meantime, Eric wasn't about to blow the opportunity he'd been waiting for by rushing the sex.

Because eleven years ago, when Deanna had started dating Marvin, Eric had felt that she had chosen the wrong brother.

Chapter 5

The next day, Deanna went to Kwame's school shortly before three-thirty as planned. She went into the office, where she saw Eric talking to the secretary. Hearing Deanna enter, he looked in her direction.

And damn if his smile didn't cause her heart to flutter.

His eyes held hers, and Deanna couldn't help wondering if he was thinking about the same thing she was.

Their kiss.

She swallowed. Just seeing those full lips, she could feel them on hers again. Who was she kidding? She didn't need to see his lips to remember the kiss.

She had relived it many times during the night.

Why hadn't someone snatched him up? Simply because he had been too busy with work? Was that his issue? There was no doubt that he was a good catch.

"Hey," he said, walking toward her.

Deanna wasn't sure if he was going to hug her, but she

darted her gaze in the direction of the secretary, a silent way of saying she wasn't sure a hug would be appropriate here. Not now that Eric had changed the landscape of their relationship by telling her that he'd always been attracted to her.

And whether he simply caught her meaning, or didn't plan to hug her regardless, he kept his hands at his side. He simply said, "It's good to see you again."

"I'm glad to be here. I'm excited to work with the kids."

Eric nodded. "Let me take you to the auditorium. The rehearsals will just be starting, so this is a good time for me to take you in and introduce you to everybody."

Deanna followed Eric the short distance from the office to the large double doors she remembered from her childhood.

And as she had thought upon seeing the exterior of her old school, the auditorium that had once seemed large and daunting didn't seem nearly as big now. Oh, it was definitely a good size, but it certainly looked smaller from her perspective as an adult.

At the end of the seating area was a stage. Deanna could remember performing Christmas and Easter plays there.

A number of kids were seated in the front row, and Deanna could only see the backs of their heads. An Indian man in jeans and a short-sleeved dress shirt sat on the edge of the stage with his feet hanging over.

"If I didn't call your name, you can still have a part in the chorus," the man was saying, "but I've made my decisions about the lead roles, and my decisions are final."

As Deanna and Eric walked down the sloping floor toward the stage, the man stopped speaking. Eric moved forward with purpose, and as he got close enough to the stage, he said, "Mr. Singh, this is Ms. Hart."

Mr. Singh hopped off of the stage and walked toward Deanna with his hand outstretched. When he reached her, he shook hers firmly. "Call me Sanjay."

"Hello, Sanjay. I'm Deanna."

Sanjay Singh looked to be in his late forties or early fifties, and he had a stern look about him.

That sternness was proven when, a moment later, he whipped his head to the right and said, "I won't tolerate any excessive chatter. No one speaks until I say otherwise."

Inwardly, Deanna cringed. For a man working on a theater production, he seemed to be tightly wound.

Then Sanjay turned back to her. "So, you're a professional recording artist. Sorry, I never heard of you."

It was the kind of comment that Deanna suspected was intended to knock her down a notch. And Eric must have figured the same thing, because he clamped a hand down on Sanjay's shoulder and said with humor, "Don't mind him. Sanjay's been living under a rock for the past decade."

The kids snickered at the comment.

"I didn't mean to come off as crass," Sanjay quickly explained, duly put in his place. "It's just that I don't keep up on current music. I'm a classical fan."

"Classical music is great," Deanna said, trying to put him at ease. But she was a little on guard, getting the sense that Sanjay wasn't exactly happy to see her.

"And that's exactly why I figured that Ms. Hart's expertise would be invaluable to you with regards to this production," Eric said. "Especially since you're filling in for Peter."

Sanjay nodded. "Yes, of course."

Eric moved to stand in front of all the students. "I'm excited about this production, and I hope you are, too. And because Mr. Guy can't be here, I thought I'd ask an old friend of mine to help out with the musical end of the production. She's had success in the music industry, with two albums released. Some of you may have heard of her." Eric paused, then grinned as he said, "Ladies and gentlemen, this is Deanna Hart."

Eric gestured to her, and Deanna stepped forward. The kids had already been throwing curious glances in her direction, some of them whispering amongst each other despite Sanjay's stern warning. She knew that at least some of the kids had recognized her.

Now, as she stepped in front of them, most were smiling excitedly, while some appeared to be blushing. "Hello," she said to them. "Nice to meet you all."

There was a chorus of hellos in return, and some of the kids waved and giggled.

"I've never worked on a Broadway production," Deanna began, "but I have done some theater—right here at this very school. And I know music. So I'm really looking forward to working with you all."

One of the kids made a funnel around his mouth with his hands and hooted, indicating his happiness over this news.

"Now," Eric went on, "this may not be Broadway, but I know you all can do a fantastic job. Working with Mr. Singh and Ms. Hart, you're going to put on the best production of *Annie* that Cleveland has ever seen!"

The students clapped and cheered in agreement.

Eric stepped to the side, and Sanjay moved to stand in front of the students again. "Okay, kids. Settle down. Time to get back to work. You all have your scripts. What we're going to do is a dry-read so everyone is familiar with their lines."

Eric stepped close to Deanna, close enough that she could smell his cologne. And though she was in a school auditorium with about twenty students, her mind transported her back to the sidewalk in front of A Taste of Soul. Suddenly she wanted Eric to snake his arms around her waist again and give her another one of those hot kisses....

"I'm going to leave you to it," Eric said to her. "But don't leave without coming to my office," he added, his voice low, and all Deanna could think was that his words were a seductive invitation.

What was wrong with her?

Sanjay started for the stage. "Ms. Hart, let me get you a script."

"Actually, I'll be right back. I just want to walk Eric out."

When they exited the auditorium, Deanna turned to Eric and said without preamble, "Are you sure this is a good idea? I have to say, Mr. Singh doesn't seem too happy to see me."

"Sanjay has become a little jaded in more recent years," Eric explained. "He's always been a little difficult, but more so lately. It's one of the reasons I think it will be good for you to work with him. The kids will benefit from having someone like you to counterbalance Sanjay. Might even be good for Sanjay himself."

"If you're sure…" Deanna said with a shrug.

"I'm definitely sure," Eric said. "Leave Sanjay to me."

Deanna returned to the auditorium, where she found the kids on stage with scripts in hand. Sanjay was standing in front of them, explaining a bit about the play and that they would simply be reading it from beginning to end today without any concern for the music.

Deanna took a seat in the front row, deciding to observe for now. Since the students were just doing a dry-read of the material, Sanjay likely wouldn't need her input today.

As suspected, Deanna wasn't needed in terms of any musical capacity at the rehearsal, and she was happy to watch and get a feel for the students and the production.

When it was over, Deanna promised Mr. Singh that she would be there the next day at 3:20. He planned to have the students begin practicing the musical numbers and would definitely need her input.

That decided, Deanna did what Eric had asked. She headed to the office to see him.

The school secretary, Michelle, wasn't behind the counter, and Deanna assumed she had left for the day. She didn't immediately see Eric, but she crossed the room to his office door, which was ajar, and knocked.

"Come in," Eric called.

Deanna found that her heart was beating more rapidly as she went through the door. Eric, who was sitting behind his desk, looked up and met her with a smile.

Deanna's breath caught in her chest. What was it about his smile that made her insides get all warm and gooey?

"Close the door," Eric said, pushing his chair back to stand.

Deanna did as instructed. And the moment the door clicked shut, Eric did something that she didn't expect. He closed the distance between them and slipped his arm around her waist.

Though the door was closed, Deanna threw a nervous glance over her shoulder. "What are you doing?"

"I missed you," Eric said.

"You saw me an hour ago," Deanna pointed out.

"That doesn't mean I can't miss you."

Warmth was spreading through her body. Though Eric's interest in her was out of the blue, Deanna couldn't deny that she was enjoying how he was making her feel. His attention was making her feel beautiful, and giddy.

Eric lowered his face to hers, but he didn't kiss her. Instead, he nuzzled his nose against hers. Then he said, "Tell me you haven't thought about kissing me again."

The words held a hint of a challenge, a challenge to prove him wrong. But Deanna couldn't do that. Because since he had kissed her yesterday, she had thought about the kiss countless times.

And yes, there was a big part of her that wanted to experience it again.

But despite that, she said, "Eric, what are you doing?"

Holding her, he rocked her body back and forth slightly. "I just want to know…have you thought about being like this with me again?"

"Are you sure you should be doing this—in your office?"

His nose moved to the underside of her jaw. "Does that mean you're not going to answer me?"

A rush of heat consumed Deanna's body. Clearly, his touch was stimulating her. She'd have to be a fool not to want to kiss him again.

But she wasn't naive enough to believe that what she was feeling was anything but lust. For one thing, the attraction had come out of the blue. She hadn't felt it nine years ago. Sure, she liked Eric, always had, but this…this was different. The other thing that made her certain she was experiencing carnal hunger was the fact that his kiss had evoked the most intense sexual reaction in her that she could remember.

She was lusting after him. She'd have to be dead not to feel a reaction to him on a physical level.

"Hmm?" Eric prompted.

A heavy breath slipped from her lips. Damn the man, he was flicking his tongue over her skin, and it was making her crazy. "I—I can't tell you that… The kiss… I enjoyed it. And I've definitely thought—" Powerless against the sensations his tongue was eliciting, she mewled. "Good God, Eric, what are you trying to do to me?"

Deanna felt Eric's lips form a smile against her skin. Then he moved them from her neck up to her jaw and slowly forward to her own mouth.

And then, right there in the office, he kissed her again.

His mouth moved over hers in a slow and sensual dance that made her stomach flutter with anticipation. His lips teased hers, coaxed hers into compliance, made her forget that only a moment ago she'd believed that acting on their lust would only lead to disaster. She was being pulled into a pit of desire, unable to stop it.

Deanna moaned against his mouth, her lips parting, and Eric's tongue dipped between them. It flicked over her own, and she found herself gripping his shoulders as a tidal wave of sensations swept over.

Eric deepened the kiss, his mouth widening, his tongue delving farther into her mouth. As her tongue tangled with his, heat pooled between her legs. Eric tightened his arms around her and a deep rumble sounded in his chest.

A knock sounded on the door, and Eric and Deanna jumped apart. Deanna's chest was heaving as she looked up at Eric, into his eyes, which were darkened with desire. His lips were moist from the kiss, and he slowly ran two fingers over them to dry them before he cleared his throat and headed to the door.

Opening the door, he sounded surprised as he said, "Hey, Michelle."

"Are you—" Michelle began, then stopped abruptly as her eyes landed on Deanna. "Oh, I'm sorry. I didn't mean to interrupt you."

"You didn't interrupt," Eric said. And as if to emphasize that fact, he opened the door wide.

"Hey," Deanna called to Michelle, adding a little wave. She hoped that her voice had come off as casual, because her heart was beating out of control.

Michelle was looking at her with an odd expression. Perhaps she sensed that there had been more going on behind closed doors than should have been on school property?

"How can I help you?" Eric asked.

Michelle's eyes narrowed slightly. "You forgot, didn't you?"

"Forgot…oh, that's right. Your car. I'm sorry."

"I have to be there in half an hour."

"Of course," Eric said. "No problem."

"And here," Michelle began, handing him a stack of papers. "I wanted to make sure that you had that information on Cincinnati that you requested."

"You didn't have to go home to get it," Eric told her. "It could have waited until tomorrow."

"Since I kept forgetting it at home, I figured I may as well bring it back to the school before I headed to the mechanic."

Eric nodded. "Well, thank you."

Deanna had been watching their interaction with interest, wondering what it was that Michelle had come back for. Now, Eric faced her. "I promised I'd go with Michelle to her mechanic, to give her a ride home. She has to leave her car there so it can be repaired." Then he turned back to Michelle. "If you'll just give me a minute."

"Sure," Michelle said. Looking at Deanna, she said, "See you later."

"Bye," Deanna said.

As Michelle walked away, Eric pushed the door to partially close it. Then he sauntered back over to Deanna. "I think perhaps this isn't the best place for...you know." Eric flashed a guilty smile.

"No, I think not," Deanna agreed. Though she ached to have his arms around her again. She wasn't sure why his touch felt so good, she only knew that it did.

"I was going to ask if you wanted to go for dinner again, but I completely forgot I promised to help Michelle out."

And though a part of Deanna was distinctly curious about Michelle and her intentions where Eric were concerned—because come on, couldn't she have found someone other than the school principal to give her a ride from her mechanic's shop?—she was also aware that another invitation to dinner wouldn't be simply about dinner. Saying yes to dinner again would be about saying yes to the start of a relationship.

And perhaps it was the fact that Michelle had caught them together, but Deanna was suddenly thinking with her head on straight. "Maybe it's for the best," Deanna said softly.

"Hmm?" Eric asked.

"Did you see the look on Michelle's face?" She paused briefly. "I'm working at your school now, albeit a volunteer position, but another dinner, more of…of whatever we were doing before Michelle showed up…we'd be crossing a certain line. And maybe, at least given the fact that I'm now working with your students, that's the wrong thing to do."

Eric pursed his lips. He looked conflicted. But he said, "Maybe you're right."

Hearing him acquiesce so easily made Deanna's stomach drop. For goodness' sake, what was wrong with her? Despite her own words, she wanted to feel Eric's lips on hers again.

"But God," he uttered, closing the distance between them, "I need one more kiss."

And Lord, didn't Deanna feel a thrill as he dipped his head to hers. But he didn't immediately kiss her. Instead, he skimmed his mouth across hers. A light, sensual touch that left her wanting more.

And when Deanna mewled softly, Eric grinned.

"By that response," he said, his voice low and ultra-sexy, "I take it the feeling's mutual."

"Yes," she rasped, knowing that by saying the word she was proving she was a big fat liar. How was it that a moment ago she'd told him they should stop what they were doing, and now she knew she couldn't stand the idea of heading home without one last kiss?

And then he kissed her, a soft, slow kiss that had her body burning in flames as effectively as the deeper kiss had.

"Tomorrow," he said, and walked to his desk, where he bent to lift a briefcase from the floor.

Tomorrow...

It sounded like a promise.

Chapter 6

All that evening, Deanna found herself unable to stop thinking about Eric, which on some level was disconcerting. Even when she had been in relationships with other men, she'd been able to put distance between her personal life and her career. Not that she was dealing with her career right now, but she wasn't sure why she was not able to stop thinking about someone who had been a friend in a decidedly sexual capacity.

Who was she kidding? How could she not think about sex after the kisses he'd given her? That man had skills, that was for sure.

Which only left her more perplexed as to why he was still single.

While searching online for more Harts in Georgia, her mind kept veering off track. She kept remembering the kiss…

What would have happened had Michelle not shown up when she had?

She frowned. And speaking of Michelle, was she wrong, or did the school secretary have a crush on the principal?

Deanna was clearly not concentrating on the task at hand. So she got up, stretched and then sat back down in front of her MacBook. She went back to her search for Harts in Lithonia. There were pages and pages. She had already called the first page of Harts listed, with no success. The task of finding her mother was daunting.

"But it isn't impossible," she told herself. And then she picked up the phone and dialed a number that belonged to an Angela Hart.

"Hello?" a young girl answered.

"Hello," Deanna said. "Is your mother or father home?"

She heard the girl call for her mother, and a moment later a woman said, "Hello?"

"Hi," Deanna began casually. "My name is Deanna, and I'm calling because I'm trying to locate someone. A woman named Miriam Hart. Now, I know this will seem odd, but this person is a family member, and we've fallen out of touch—"

"Sorry," the woman interjected before Deanna could finish her practiced spiel. "I don't now anyone named Miriam Hart."

"Perhaps a Mary Hart?" Deanna asked.

"No, no Mary Hart, either."

Deanna frowned. "Okay. Thanks, anyway."

As she ended the call, she emitted a groan. There were always a few moments of hope as she'd made her calls. There had been three Miriams and eleven Marys—but upon talking to those people, she had quickly determined that none of those women were her mother.

Perhaps it would be smarter to have a detective work this case. The problem was, not knowing their mother's true roots, Deanna and her sisters didn't have the best information to go on. Any detective was bound to turn up a lot of false leads.

Deanna wasn't ready to hand over the search for her mother

yet. Nigel was still working things on his end, and she could only hope that he would uncover something soon. He had already looked into the police file, and it stated that their mother's name was Miriam Hart. Either that was truthful, or she had changed her name and somehow had been able to cover her tracks. Because by following the leads in the police file, Nigel hadn't found any roots in Georgia.

Deanna had made enough calls for one evening. Come tomorrow, she would start again.

And with any luck, and a little faith, tomorrow would bring the lead she and her sisters had been praying for.

Deanna went to the school the next day at 3:20, as planned. She hoped that Mr. Singh would be more amiable today. Perhaps he had been shocked by her appearance yesterday and the news that she would be working with him on the production. Either that or he was simply having a bad day.

Some kids were already assembled on the stage as she made her way down to the front of the auditorium. Only seven, she noted, doing a quick head count. Mr. Singh was handing out scripts, which caused her brow to furrow. Hadn't he done that yesterday?

A couple of the girls waved at her, and Mr. Singh quickly turned to look over his shoulder. Seeing her, he offered her a tight smile.

Better than yesterday, but still not warm and fuzzy.

Deanna ascended the stairs onto the stage and walked toward him. He also handed her a script. "These are the musical numbers," he explained. "All of the songs with the sheet music."

"Ah," Deanna said, lifting the cover. The first song was "It's a Hard Knock Life," one of the musical's iconic songs.

"Mrs. Olney will be here with us today," Mr. Singh announced. "She'll be playing the musical numbers on the piano. Ah, there she is now."

Deanna looked over her shoulder to see a heavyset blond woman entering the auditorium. Another handful of students were also walking down the aisle.

"Everyone, come up on stage," Mr. Singh announced.

Mrs. Olney walked up onto the stage and headed for Deanna immediately. She offered her hand. "So nice to meet you. I was elated to hear you'd be helping out with the production."

"Deanna," Deanna said, formally introducing herself.

"I know."

"And your name?" Deanna asked.

"Oh, heaven's me. I'm Lucy. Lucy Olney. I'm the substitute music teacher. I'll be playing the piano."

"Ah," Deanna said. She hadn't realized the woman would be participating in the musical production, but it made sense.

"All right, everyone's here," Mr. Singh announced. "Come onto the stage. If you haven't received the book of music, please come get one from me." He passed more folders of music to the last few students. "We'll all be turning to the first page, 'It's a Hard Knock Life.' If you're not a part of the chorus, you may take a seat."

Mrs. Olney settled behind the piano. Mr. Singh instructed her to play the song in its entirety before they attempted singing along to it. Then the seven girls who were a part of the chorus sang the song in unison, getting a feel for the beat and the lyrics.

Deanna watched, taking note of which girls seemed the strongest musically and which ones would need some work. It was early, of course, but that was why she was here.

She liked that unlike the original Broadway show, the girl playing Annie in this production was African-American. And she had some ideas about how to add a more hip-hop flavor to the music to make the show more relevant and contemporary for the student body at this school, which she would broach with Mr. Singh once they got beyond the basic stage of getting familiar with the music.

All in all, the rehearsal went well, and even though some of the girls had started off more shy, most had gained confidence by the end of their time on stage.

"That was good work for today," Mr. Singh announced at the end of the rehearsal, and he sounded genuinely pleased. "Please make sure you spend the time before the next practice learning your lines. Yes, I've given out the lead roles already, but if I deem that you're not taking the part seriously, I will give it to someone else."

As Deanna got to her feet from where she had been sitting in the front row at the end of the rehearsal, a few of the kids came over to her. She had seen some of them eyeing her, especially one boy named Keith. He had looked at her several times, offering what she thought were flirtatious smiles.

It wasn't new for Deanna. Young boys and old men alike had found her attractive, and the fact that she was in the public eye also made her an appealing person to fantasize about. That was the reason she wasn't keen on showing too much flesh in her videos and public appearances, unlike some other female artists. Her manager had pointed out that that very decision had made it harder for her to top the charts. She had done well, but the wholesome, clean performers did not sell as well as the racier ones.

Keith pushed his way past the few girls walking toward her so that he got to her first. He grinned at her with a boyishly confident smile that said he knew the girls liked him.

"I think I could use some special help," Keith said to her.

"Really?" Deanna asked. "What kind of help are you interested in?"

"Well, as you know, I'm playing the part of Pepper, and

if you could help me with my upper register—I'd like to be able to sing at a higher pitch."

"Certainly. I'd be happy to give some vocal coaching exercises. In fact, maybe that's one way I can contribute," she said, more to herself. She approached Mr. Singh. "I just thought of one way I can help. I can come up with some vocal exercises to help the students before they start their rehearsals. Five to ten minutes at the beginning of each rehearsal."

Mr. Singh nodded. "Certainly. That sounds like a great idea."

Deanna smiled. And as she turned, Keith was there, towering over her. For an eighth-grader, he was quite tall.

"Would you mind?" Grinning, he extended a notepad. "If I can get an autograph, and a picture, that would be awesome."

"Certainly," Deanna said. She dutifully smiled as he held up his iPhone and took a photo of the two of them. Then she scribbled her name on the notepad he had given her. The other kids immediately followed suit, lining up for their photos, as well. Yesterday, they hadn't been prepared to get autographs and photos, but today was a different story. Deanna graciously obliged them all.

Afterward, Mr. Singh cleared his throat and clapped his hands. "Okay. You've gotten that out of the way, which is good. Because I'll have no more of that at the next rehearsal. I'm sure Ms. Hart doesn't want you fussing over her like this. From here on in, it's strictly business."

Once the kids started to file out of the room, their photos and autographs in hand, Deanna approached Mr. Singh. "That was interesting," Deanna said.

"Indeed."

She placed her hands on her hips as she looked at Mr. Singh. "I'm excited about the opportunity to work with you and the students. Looks like it's going to be fun. For me as well as the students."

"I only hope it's not a distraction."

"Excuse me?" Deanna asked.

"The kids are all a bit star struck," Mr. Singh said with a tight smile. "Which makes sense. I only hope they're not so star struck that they're distracted from doing their best."

No, Deanna thought, frowning slightly, *I didn't get it wrong yesterday. Mr. Singh isn't thrilled to have me on the production team.*

"I think they got that out of their systems today," Deanna said. "By next week, I'm just going to be a regular person. Trust me."

Mr. Singh gathered his briefcase, nodding. "I suppose. We'll see." He paused, meeting Deanna's gaze. "If Keith becomes a problem, please let me know."

"Oh, I don't think he'll be a problem." He was a little star struck, and perhaps had a little boy crush on her. Harmless. For kids like Keith, the mileage would come from being able to post pictures with her on Facebook and brag about how he had a personal connection to her.

"All the same, if he acts in a way that's inappropriate, please let me know. I'll make sure I deal with him."

"Sure," Deanna said. But she didn't like the man's tone. She could envision him clamping down an iron fist to keep the students under control. Not good, especially considering Eric had said that he'd challenged some of the students to join the drama club as a way to help them come out of their shells.

Deanna only hoped that Mr. Singh would mellow out as they continued to work together.

All the same, she was glad to utter the words, "See you next Wednesday," and be on her way. She headed to the auditorium's exit.

Once she was in the school's foyer, she stopped. She had weighed heavily her attraction to Eric and also what she'd said before they parted yesterday. That crossing a line would be the wrong thing to do, especially now. So she had planned to attend the rehearsal and head back home.

But now…

Now, she felt that perhaps leaving without even a hello would be rude.

So she found herself turning and heading in the direction of the office. No harm saying hello to a friend, right?

Michelle was still there, doing some filing or other paperwork, and Deanna said pleasantly, "Hey, Michelle."

"Hello, Ms. Hart."

"Deanna's fine." A beat. "Is Eric still here? Mr. Bell," she quickly corrected.

"Yep. In his office."

Deanna nodded, then went to the closed door and lightly rapped on it. A moment later, Eric was opening it. And as he had done the day before, his face lit up in a huge smile as he saw her. It was the kind of reaction that a woman could get used to, that was for sure.

The man was drop-dead gorgeous.

"Hello, Deanna. Come in, come in."

She stepped into the office. "Hey, Eric."

"How was the rehearsal?" Eric asked her.

"It was great," she told him. "I think it's going to be a great production."

"Glad to hear it."

She couldn't help but notice that Eric didn't close the door this time, and she felt a little disappointed. Which made no sense at all. She was the one who'd pointed out that they needed to stop any hanky-panky, especially at school.

It was just that seeing him again had already set her pulse racing.

He rested his butt against the edge of the desk, and then he simply stared at her. "Do me a favor?"

"Hmm?"

"Dinner."

"Dinner?" Deanna repeated.

Eric gestured for her to step forward, and when she did, he said in a lowered voice, "I know what you said yesterday, but I have to tell you, just seeing you again…" His voice trailed off, and when he spoke again, his voice was barely above a whisper. "Just seeing you again, I want nothing more than to kiss you."

Deanna's heart slammed against her chest. Good Lord, she wanted the same thing. Her brain might be telling her that she and Eric should continue on the friendship path, that acting on their lust would be a bad idea. But every time she saw him, her hormones went into overdrive.

"And if I'm going to kiss you again, it can't be here. So say yes to dinner. There's a quaint little spot—"

"Yes," Deanna said softly. Because no matter what her brain told her, her desire was dictating her actions now. And she definitely wanted to kiss Eric again.

"We can head out now," Eric told her.

"Works for me," Deanna said. She was dressed in jeans and a blouse and low-heeled boots…more than appropriate for dinner.

Eric lifted his briefcase. "You can follow me to the restaurant. Or we can go together, and I'll take you back here afterward."

"I'll follow you," Deanna said.

Eric led the way out of the office and then out the school's front doors. Soon, he was approaching a late-model gold Ford Explorer.

"My car's right over there," Deanna said, pointing. "The red Porsche."

Eric whistled lowly. "Wow. Nice car."

Deanna grinned. Eric hadn't seen the car when they'd left A Taste of Soul, because she'd insisted on rounding the corner to her parked car independently. Which she had done because she knew that if he'd followed her there, she would have been far too tempted to invite herself back to his place.

"Yeah," Deanna said, "it was my first splurge purchase when I released my first album. It was in L.A. until last month, when I went back to get it and drive it here."

"So you're staying for a while." Eric's voice rose on a hopeful note.

"For the time be—"

Her word died in her throat when Eric suddenly reached for her arm and pulled her against him. And then he planted his lips on hers.

"Eric," Deanna said, easing her body backward, her breathing coming in gasps. "We're still at your school."

"I know." He groaned softly and ran a hand down her arm.

Deanna gazed at him suspiciously, still unable to believe who this man was. Years ago, he had been nothing but the supportive brother of her boyfriend. He had shown none of this side, the side that was clearly interested in something with her. It had come out of left field.

And yet, she was enjoying it.

"We're leaving," he said. "As soon as I do this…"

Leaning forward, Eric's mouth found her jaw line and skimmed her skin from there to the base of her neck. Deanna moaned as the feelings of pleasure came over her.

It had been too long since she'd enjoyed a man's touch. That was her problem. Too long since she'd felt a burning passion like this. In fact, she never had—at least not this intensely.

"Damn," Eric mumbled. "Okay. Let's get out of here."

He turned, and as if Deanna's hand had a mind of its own, it reached out and stroked Eric's back.

Whirling around, he eyed her with a pleasantly surprised look. "Gosh…I…" Deanna didn't know what to say. She'd just touched Eric in the manner of a woman who was making a sexual advance.

What is wrong with me?

Eric winked at her. "Yeah, let's get out of here."

Chapter 7

Eric got into his vehicle, and, her heart pounding wildly, Deanna headed to hers. She couldn't believe what she'd just done.

Yes, she had always felt comfortable around Eric, but so much so that she'd reached out to stroke him like that?

Comprehending her lust for the man was baffling, but she tried to put it out of her mind as she followed him out of the parking lot. Eric turned onto the city street and drove for a few minutes before abruptly pulling to the right and stopping. Deanna did the same, confused as to why he was pulling over here.

As Eric exited his vehicle and approached her car, Deanna couldn't help noting just how sexy he was. He had the kind of athletic physique that made a woman take a second look. And the sleek sunglasses he had donned had only added to his sex appeal.

She put her window down. "Yes?"

He leaned in to her window, resting an arm on the ledge, and Deanna couldn't help wondering if he was going to kiss her again.

"Something just came up," Eric said.

Deanna narrowed her eyes. "Since the time we left the school?"

"We should have exchanged numbers," he said. "That way I could have called you instead of stopping like this. But I just got a call." He pursed his lips. "And I have to go take care of something."

His tone was serious. "Everything okay?"

"I'm not sure. It's one of my students. She's been having some difficulties at home—some domestic problems. I told her she could call me whenever she needed me. She just did."

"Oh." Deanna frowned slightly. "Okay, we can do dinner another time."

"Actually, I want you to come with me. If you don't mind. I shouldn't be that long. Risha is apparently at her neighbor's house, and I plan to go there and contact the police if need be."

"The police—oh, my. Did she say what was going on?"

"Only that she's scared. Her father is an alcoholic," Eric explained. "He can be volatile."

"Are you sure you should be heading over there?" Deanna asked. "If the father can be volatile…"

"I'm not sure what's going on," Eric said. "But I told Risha she could call me anytime." He paused. "I still want to have dinner with you, though. This will just be a little detour. Will you come with me?"

"If you really want me to."

"I do."

Eric got back into his Ford, signaled a left turn and then did a U-turn. He headed back in the direction from where they had been coming.

A few minutes later, after making a series of turns into

a neighborhood, Eric pulled his vehicle to a stop in front of a small white house. Deanna was relieved to see that there was no commotion outside, and turning off her engine, she heard no sounds other than the chirping of birds and slow-moving traffic.

Eric got out of the car, and Deanna, unsure, did the same. She figured that if nothing else, once she got to the house and learned the problem, she could call Nigel directly and ask him for advice or perhaps have him tend to the matter.

Eric walked toward her. "You may as well wait here while I go and find out what's going on."

Deanna nodded. "Sure."

She watched as he went to the front door and knocked. Then, and a moment later, when a woman answered, she watched him disappear into the house.

Deanna eased her butt against her car and waited, watching the house's front door and worrying. Eric had said that Risha had gone to a neighbor's house, so her eyes volleyed between the door Eric had entered and the houses on either side of it.

Nothing happened.

Several minutes later, when Deanna saw the door of the house Eric had entered begin to open, she quickly stood up straight. Eric stepped onto the porch with the little girl who must have been Risha and the middle-aged woman who had opened the door. The girl was crying, her shoulders shaking with each emotional sob.

Oh, that poor girl. It broke Deanna's heart.

And suddenly she felt a jolt as though she had just been struck by a live wire. Her nightmare came back to her. The man striking the woman. The woman falling to the ground.

Deanna spun around. Her chest was constricting, making it hard to breathe. Closing her eyes, she hugged her torso.

She jumped when she felt the hand on her back. And when she turned, she looked into Eric's concerned eyes.

"Hey," Eric said softly. "Are you okay?"

Deanna nodded. "I just…that poor little girl…"

Eric was giving her an odd look. "You don't look okay."

"Don't worry about me." She forced a smile. "What's happening with Risha?"

"Her father was drinking. Then he went into a rage. He beat Risha's mother and when she grabbed Risha who was nearby and ran out of the house to the neighbor's, he fled. Thankfully he didn't follow them there, but his car isn't in the driveway, which means he took off while drunk." Eric shook his head in dismay. "I just convinced Risha's mother to call the police, so they're on their way."

Deanna shivered—and it had nothing to do with the slight breeze. Again, her eyes were drawn to the little girl, standing on the porch, crying inconsolably.

What was it about that visual that bothered her so much—other than the obvious?

It was her dream. And the memory of what Brian had done to her.

"Your mother's going to be fine," the woman, who now had her arms wrapped around Risha, was telling her.

Eric placed both hands on her shoulders. "Deanna, you look as though you've seen a ghost."

She jerked her gaze to his. "I do?"

"Yeah."

"I don't know, Eric. I'm kind of thinking that maybe I should just go home."

"No. Look, forget about dinner out at a restaurant. I'm taking you to my place. You're not all right."

Gone was the flirtatious side to him. Instead, he was eyeing her with concern.

Deanna nodded. She didn't want to be alone. She wanted the friend who had always been there for her in her hour of need when she'd had her problems with Marvin. Because obviously the situation the little girl was facing had brought her back to that ugly place with Brian, causing her to relive her own experience with domestic abuse.

"Come on," Eric told her, putting his hand around her shoulder. "You need to sit on the porch."

As Eric led Deanna up the walkway, the woman took Risha into the house. No sooner than Eric was placing Deanna on one of the wicker chairs, the police cruiser pulled up in front of the house.

Two officers—one male and one female—exited the police car. Good, Deanna thought when she saw the female. Risha might prefer talking to a woman about what had happened.

Eric met them as they were coming up the walkway and briefly explained what was going on. Then the officers entered the house. A moment later, the female cop exited with Risha and asked her what had happened.

The male cop had stayed inside with Risha's mother. Yes, it made sense that they would want to get two independent accounts of what had happened.

"My daddy was acting crazy," Risha said. No longer crying, she was speaking clearly. Bravely. "He kept yelling and screaming. And then he hurt my mommy."

Deanna ached to put her arms around Risha, tell her that everything would be okay.

The man striking the woman. The woman falling to the ground.

"Sometimes, my daddy drinks too much," Risha added in a sad tone. "Is my mommy going to be okay?"

"She's going to be fine," the officer assured her. "There's an ambulance coming to take her to the hospital. I don't want you to be scared by that. The doctors are just going to check your mom out, make sure that she's totally okay."

Risha nodded.

"How old is she?" Deanna asked quietly. "She looks about nine, the same age as Kwame."

"She's ten," Eric answered. "And she's in Kwame's class."

Kwame would be turning ten next month. Ten was far too young for someone to be dealing with something as horrible as domestic abuse.

It took only another minute for the ambulance to arrive. Deanna didn't know how badly Risha's mother was hurt, but she hardly breathed as she watched the paramedics head into the house with a stretcher. A short while later they exited with the woman on a gurney. Her bottom lip was busted and swollen, and her face was bloodied.

"Oh, my God," Deanna exclaimed as the paramedics made their way down the steps with the injured woman. Her stomach lurched.

The woman was crying, and Eric immediately went to her. "Please—Jeffrey didn't mean it. He just…he had too much to drink."

So typical, Deanna thought sadly. Her husband had beat her horribly, and yet she didn't want to see him charged.

She herself had walked away from Brian, rather than press charges.

The man striking the woman. The woman falling to the ground.

Deanna's head throbbed.

"Don't you worry about that," Eric said as the gurney reached the ambulance. "You're going to the hospital. The doctors are going to make sure you're okay."

Perhaps because she knew she had no other choice, the woman didn't refuse. But Deanna got the sense that she wanted to jump off of the stretcher.

"Thank you for coming, Mr. Bell," she said. "Thank you for being there for my baby."

"Of course," Eric said.

Risha reached for her mother's hand and only released it so that the paramedics could load her into the ambulance. Then Risha climbed in, as well.

Deanna watched as Eric stayed at the ambulance doors until they were closed. And all she could think was that he was the same chivalrous Eric she had known as a teenager, the strong man whom the damsel in distress could lean on. She had always loved that about him.

Once the ambulance drove off, Eric went to the neighbor and said a few words. Something to the effect of thanking her for being there for Risha and her mother, from what she could hear. Then he went back to her and pulled her against him. "You okay?"

"I'm okay. It's just…that was disturbing."

"Of course it was." He kissed her temple. "You're coming to my house, right? You look really shaken up."

"Sure," she replied.

"You okay to follow me?" Eric asked her.

Deanna nodded shakily. "Yeah."

They got into their vehicles, and Deanna followed Eric. It turned out that he lived about twenty minutes out of Fairfax, the middle-class neighborhood where the school was and where they had all lived as kids. Eric was still in East Cleveland but in the neighborhood of Glenville.

Deanna pulled into the driveway behind his car. She was exiting her Porsche when he came over to meet her. And then, as if he had done it thousands of times, he placed his hand on the small of her back and guided her to his front door.

The exterior of the house, painted in a deep burgundy with white accents, looked to have been recently renovated. There was a wide porch with a swing large enough for two. It was the kind of dwelling that could easily house a few kids.

Deanna's eyes homed in on the door's colorful stained-glass insert as Eric opened it. Then she followed him into a spacious foyer. The next moment, she gasped in fright when she saw that a black fur ball was charging down the staircase toward them.

"Oh," she said, placing a hand on her chest as she realized what it was. "It's a cat."

The cat, which upon closer inspection Deanna saw had brown markings mixed in with the black, rubbed against Eric's leg and then went to her and did the same.

"This is Sadie," he said, bending to scratch the cat behind the ears. "She's a tortoiseshell. You're not allergic, are you?"

"No." Deanna shook her head.

Eric narrowed his eyes as he looked at her. Then he placed both hands on Deanna's shoulders. "You told me you were okay, but you look far from okay. What's going on?"

Deanna drew in a deep breath, wondering if she wanted to get into what had happened. But hadn't she trusted Eric with all of her problems years ago?

"I guess…I guess it's just that what happened with that little girl reminded me of something that happened to me."

Eric made a face. "What does that mean?"

"Maybe we can sit down?"

"Of course," Eric said, gesturing to the living room. It was an open-concept living and dining space, and though the house was likely decades old, the interior boasted modern furnishings as well as modern fixtures.

Deanna strolled to the cream-colored leather sectional. By the time she sank into it, Sadie was right there, jumping up onto her lap to demand attention.

"Sorry," Eric said. "She's very affectionate."

"Don't apologize." She stroked the cat's back. "I love cats. They're independent and can mostly take care of themselves—the perfect pet for me. I had one in L.A., but it went out one day and never returned."

Eric took a seat beside her. "That's why Sadie's an indoor

cat." He stroked his pet, and then it jumped off of Deanna's lap and went over to a multilevel cat scratching pad and jumped up onto the first level.

"So," Eric said, looking into her eyes. "Tell me what's going on."

Deanna inhaled a deep breath and released it slowly. It was amazing how painful this was to talk about. Maybe it was as much about feeling like a fool for having dated Brian and trusting him as it was about what he'd done to her.

"Deanna?" Eric prompted.

"It's just… I was dating someone at the beginning of the year. A music producer." She scowled. "I thought he was my chance to get back on the scene. Help me produce a new album. One thing led to another, and we started dating. But when I realized that we would be better off concentrating on business as opposed to getting personal, that's when…that's when he lost it."

"What did he do?" Eric asked, his tone grave.

"He hit me." There was no sugarcoating what Brian had done.

"He put his hands on you?" Eric's nostrils flared. "Did you go to the police?"

Deanna shook her head. She felt a little ashamed about the fact that she had simply tried to avoid him, cut him out of her life, and had ultimately let him get away with what he'd done. "I didn't want that headache. I didn't want the media attention. I just…I just wanted him to be gone. Out of my life."

"But he hurt you. Obviously, he hurt you enough that this incident today is triggering a huge reaction in you. I've never seen you look so unsettled."

She turned away from him, thinking about just how uncomfortable she felt.

No, it wasn't simply discomfort. She felt anxiety.

"Hey," Eric said, placing a gentle hand on her arm. "What exactly did he do?"

"I told him I thought it was best that we concentrate on our working relationship, that being involved was clouding our ability to get work done. Before we started dating, he seemed like an easygoing guy. A dedicated professional. But it's like he felt that once we were an item, he had a license to know everything I was up to. He'd be jealous about other men I met, wonder where I was all the time. It wasn't even like we were all that serious."

"It doesn't matter if you were engaged to be married. He didn't have a right to put his hands on you."

"I know," Deanna said, sighing. "I just keep wishing I'd never gotten involved with him. I know this is going to sound stupid, but in hindsight I can't deny that I thought us being a couple would be a good thing for my career. I liked him— don't get me wrong. But I was looking at the big picture. And in my mind, I was seeing us as another music super-couple. But I quickly realized that I was more interested in getting my next album done than being involved with him. So I tried to let him down gently, because I definitely still wanted to work with him. But he didn't take it well. He got rough with me. Grabbed me. Squeezed my arms so hard that he left bruises. When I tried to get away from him, he slapped me—though maybe it was a punch. All I know is that he hit me in the face twice. Like Risha's mother, I ended up with a busted lip."

Eric slowly rose to his feet, and Deanna could see the tension in his body. He was livid.

He paced the hardwood floor, his fists clenching. Then he faced Deanna again. "And he got away with this?"

"I just wanted it to be over."

"I have a mind to head out to Hollywood right now. Teach him a lesson for daring to put his hands on you."

Deanna actually found the courage to smile. The fact that Eric was so moved to defend her meant the world to her.

Deanna got to her feet and stepped toward him. She placed a hand on his chest. "As much as I would love for you to do that, I realized it was best to let it go with Brian. Cut him out of my life and be done with him."

"He should have been charged."

"It's done."

"Is it?" Eric asked. "Guys like that—jealous guys— sometimes they can't let a woman go."

"Well…" Deanna's voice trailed off. Eric was right. Brian hadn't been able to let it go. But neither had he been willing to bust down her door to get to her. So he'd done the next best thing—trashed her in the industry. Soon, Deanna's agent had dumped her, and her calls to the music label she and Brian had been working with had gone unanswered. Word had gotten back to her afterward that her reputation had been smeared.

"He got nasty," she said. "That's how he lashed out at me. I think he knew better than to come to my door and physically go after me again, because then I would have called the police. He called and called, and when I didn't respond to him, he attacked my reputation. It's one of the reasons coming here after my aunt passed was a godsend. It allowed me to take a break from all that ugliness."

"So he trashed your reputation?"

Deanna shrugged nonchalantly, though she knew Brian's actions had been far from casual. "Let's just say I'm taking this time to figure out what I really want to do with my life."

"Deanna." Eric shook his head.

"I don't want to talk about Brian anymore," Deanna said, slipping her arms around Eric's waist.

His eyes widened in surprise. Even the cat mewed, as though startled by the sudden action.

She knew he had to be wondering why she had gone from

talking about something so heavy to trying to be amorous. But she was tired of taking this trip down memory lane. "Weren't you the one who talked about silver linings?"

"Yeah," he said, but the word sounded like a question.

Now that her arms were wrapped around his strong waist, she wanted nothing more than to feel his lips on hers again. To lose herself in the sensation of something wonderful, as opposed to remembering the disturbing memories of the past.

"Well…I'd like to think that reconnecting with you is a silver lining." Her voice was husky, and she had to wonder exactly what she was doing. It was as if her mouth and body had a mind of their own.

Because she knew Eric had to be thinking that she was trying to seduce him.

He stared down at her with a question in his eyes, and she could feel the rise and fall of his chest against hers. "I can't say that I'm not happy to have you here. Selfishly, I'm glad you're not back in L.A. So, yeah, that's a silver lining. But still, this Brian guy—"

"Shhh. Let's just take this as fate. Maybe some things are happening the way they're supposed to happen."

She held his gaze, and he held hers, neither breathing, letting their desire speak for itself.

"Deanna…"

Placing a finger on his lips, she eased herself up onto her toes, letting him know that she wanted to kiss him. "No more talking," she told him.

And then she reached her head forward and pressed her mouth against Eric's. She sighed against his lips almost instantly, heat immediately spreading through her body. She wasn't exactly sure what it was about this man that drew her to him so greatly; she only knew that with him she felt beautiful.

And safe. She knew Eric would never hurt her.

So what could it hurt to explore the sexual feelings she was having for him?

He tore his lips from hers. "Deanna…what are you…?"

His voiced trailed off, ending on a groan when she nibbled on the underside of his jaw. "Why do you keep talking?" she asked softly.

"Damn, what are you doing to me?" His voice was low and throaty, and Deanna could hear the warring emotions in him. "We're about to cross that line you said we shouldn't cross…."

"Which you didn't seem to care all that much about to begin with," she pointed out. "Why don't we, at least for now, forget that I ever talked to you about any restrictive line? Because I think it's fair to say that we've both been ignoring it."

She nibbled again, and Deanna knew the moment Eric succumbed to her charms. A lustful growl escaped his lips, and then his arms went around her waist with force. Holding her to him tightly, he planted his lips on hers.

And then fire consumed them both.

Chapter 8

Eric kissed Deanna ferociously, his need for her all-consuming. There was a small part in his brain that was confused, unsure how they had gone from her being distressed to kissing as though both of their lives depended on it. But the overwhelming part of him was feeling explosive desire.

Her hands moved up his back, and…man, her touch—it was the very thing Eric had fantasized about years ago.

And several times since her departure.

He pulled her closer, splaying his fingers over the curve of her back. She moaned softly and dug her fingers into his shoulder blades as he pressed his arousal against her.

"Yes, Eric…"

The small part of Eric's brain that wondered how they had gotten to this point so fast began to consume more of his thoughts. And as much as he didn't want to, he found himself pulling his lips from hers.

"I don't know, Deanna. One minute you weren't okay. And now—"

"Now, I'm very okay. Trust me."

She hadn't been drinking. But that didn't mean her faculties were in good working order.

Grief and anxiety could cause people to act in ways they otherwise wouldn't.

When Deanna's hands went down to his butt and squeezed, Eric took the opportunity to reach for her hands and pull them away from his body.

Narrowing her eyes in confusion, she looked up at him.

"This isn't…it's not right," he told her.

Eric couldn't do this. Not right now. Not while it seemed to him that Deanna was turning to him for comfort.

Oh, he very much wanted to make love to her. But he wanted to know that she wanted him—not an escape from whatever bad memories were assailing her.

So with difficulty, Eric took a step backward, hoping to break the spell his body was under.

"I definitely want to," Eric went on. "And maybe I'm going to regret this the moment you're gone. But I respect you too much to go from having you crying about Brian to you being in my bed."

Call him excessively old-fashioned, but he hadn't taken advantage of Deanna when he could have back when she'd been grieving over Marvin. And perhaps had he tried to, she would have been willing to seek sexual comfort in his arms. But he had respected her too much to do that then, and he sure as hell respected her too much to do that now.

Even if she was begging him to do it.

Eric watched Deanna's chest rise and fall as her gaze held his. She seemed confused. Or perhaps disappointed. But after a moment, she began to nod.

"You're right. I would probably regret this tomorrow." She continued to nod. "No, you're absolutely right."

"Like I said, it's not that I don't want to…"

"But you've always been nothing if not a gentleman," Deanna told him, her lips curling in a small smile.

"I couldn't feel good about myself if I thought I took advantage of you."

"No," Deanna agreed. "You couldn't." Sighing, she hugged her arms to her body. "I suppose I ought to get going."

"I'm not kicking you out," Eric said. " I promised you dinner, and I'm happy to deliver. If you give me about an hour to cook."

"A man who cooks," Deanna said in a sing-song voice. "I can't believe a woman hasn't already snatched you up."

Eric's jaw flinched. There were times when he wondered about the same thing. But he had come to learn that no matter how many women claimed they wanted a nice guy, they were far more willing to date the jerks.

"The chicken's already seasoned. It's my mother's Southern fried chicken recipe, which I guarantee you'll love."

"Mmm, sounds delicious." Then Deanna cocked her head to the side as she regarded him. "Speaking of your mother— where are your parents?"

"They moved to Cincinnati," Eric told her, and he felt his heart catch in his chest. In many ways, he had to wonder why Deanna had shown up now. Considering what he was trying to set in motion. If he was hired at the school in Cincinnati, he would be leaving soon. And it was definitely too soon in this phase of trying to get to know Deanna on a deeper level for him to expect her to move with him.

"Cincinnati," she repeated.

"Yep. They moved there so they could see their grandchildren more readily. Since that's where Beverly now lives with her new husband."

"And didn't your school secretary say something to you about Cincinnati?"

"Yeah." Eric nodded, his lips in a tight line. Should he tell her? Did it even matter at this point? Deanna had roots here, but she wasn't tied to Cleveland. She had moved to L.A. for a number of years, after all.

And wouldn't that be where she returned once she had the loose ends in her life here tied up?

"I've been looking into possibly changing gears myself," he told her. "There's an opportunity to work with an Afrocentric school in Cincinnati."

"Really?"

Eric detected a hint of something in Deanna's eyes, but it could've just been his own imagination. Lord knew he wanted her to react to what he'd told her. He wanted to hear her say that she wasn't ready for him to walk out of her life already.

"They're considering me to be a principal of the school, as well as hold a position on the board," Eric explained. "I love the vision of the educators trying to set this in motion. And the opportunity to work with kids who feel displaced in the traditional school system. The job would start in January. But I'm not sure if I'll take the position, even if it's offered to me."

"It sounds like an important position," Deanna said. "And the fact that they're considering you when you live in Cleveland…your reputation is obviously stellar."

"I know one of the people working on getting the school going. And yes, he and the others are impressed with the work I've done. Not just as a principal, but as a teacher. I'm able to reach a lot of kids who would otherwise be lost. I'm not bragging—I feel blessed for this to be my calling. The thing is, I also love my work here. So I'm not entirely sure what I'm going to do."

Though the truth was, until Deanna had shown up at his school in Cleveland, he had seen no reason to stay here. His parents were now in Cincinnati, not to mention his nephew and niece.

But now…

Eric no longer wanted to discuss this topic, so he started toward his dining room, from where he would exit into the kitchen. "I'm going to get dinner started. Feel free to turn on the television."

In the kitchen, Eric turned the oven on and then got the chicken from the fridge. As he began to coat the boneless pieces in flour, he heard the television come on.

A short while later, Deanna came into the kitchen. "I don't feel right sitting on the sofa waiting for you to prepare a meal for me. Tell me how I can help."

"You can peel the potatoes. I was going to make a potato salad."

"Then you're in luck. Because I make a mean potato salad."

They fell into a rhythm in the kitchen, and Eric couldn't help smiling inside. It was nice having her here. She fit into his space with ease.

"Where's the pot you want me to put the potatoes in?"

Eric crossed from the stove to a cupboard near the sink, which he opened and then withdrew a large pot. "Here."

"Thanks," Deanna said. She took the pot from him, then turned on the faucet and began to fill it with water.

"By the way." Eric rested his butt against the counter and looked at her. "I've got a wedding to go to on Saturday. I rsvp'd for two, but I'm going with a couple of friends and didn't have anyone I wanted to ask. I know it's short notice, but I'd love it if you would be my official date."

"Wow. You weren't kidding when you said it was short notice."

"Do you have plans?"

"No. No plans."

"Will you join me?"

"Sure."

Eric held Deanna's gaze for a long moment. He couldn't read what she was thinking, but she offered him a small smile and then headed toward the stove.

Eric watched her, his eyes moving over her from head to toe. She was fit. It was obvious she worked out to stay in shape, but not so much that she didn't have any womanly curves. Her butt looked amazing in her jeans.

Everything about her was utterly sexy. And when she had her body pressed against his and his arms around her waist, it had taken all of his willpower to turn her down.

His friend Hector would tell him he was a fool for not having taken advantage of what Deanna had been offering. Hector thought that Eric was wasting his time waiting for the one right woman, rather than enjoying the smorgasbord of females the good Lord had provided.

All Eric knew was that come Saturday night, if Deanna was still willing, it would be a whole other story.

Just over an hour later, Deanna was sitting with Eric at his maple dining room table. He had a large house, and he lived there alone. Deanna couldn't help reflecting that he must feel lonely.

"You like living here?" she asked.

"It's a nice house, a nice neighborhood."

"But you've got all this space just for yourself."

"And it must get lonely?"

Deanna nodded as she ate a mouthful of chicken. "That's what I was thinking."

"I bought this as an investment after Ellie and I divorced. It needed extensive renovations, but now it's worth more than twice what I paid for it."

"Did you do the renovations?"

"Only a few small things. I'm smart enough to know where my strengths are, so I contracted most of the work out."

"Well, the place looks wonderful." The marble kitchen counters were tan with black flecks and went well with the warm colors in his home. The beige-colored backsplash added a sophisticated touch. It was the kind of kitchen a person would enjoy cooking in, and Deanna had certainly enjoyed doing so with Eric.

"Thanks."

"And I suppose you might be moving sooner than you know. If this opportunity in Cincinnati comes through."

Eric sipped some of his white wine. "We'll see," he said noncommittally.

"By the way, my compliments to the chef. This chicken is delicious."

Now his face lit up. "I knew you'd like it."

"And thank you for dinner," Deanna went on. "I think this was just what I needed." She didn't quite meet his eyes as she said the last words, because she was thinking about how she had thrown herself at Eric, and if not for his resolve, she would have ended up in his bed.

At least Eric was insightful enough to know that had she done that, she may very well have regretted it in the morning. And not just because she would have been seeking a reprieve from her pain. But she was still battling with her lust for him. She could sleep with him, yes, but then what? He was talking about moving to Cincinnati, and she would likely end up back in Los Angeles.

In other words, if she went to bed with Eric, there would be no promise of tomorrow.

And that was the kicker. Because while they clearly had a strong physical attraction for each other, sleeping with him could lead to the end of their friendship. Considering Deanna's track record with men, it only made sense to keep her friendship with Eric intact.

"So," Eric began, interrupting her thoughts, "what's up with your career now? Now that this Brian guy has tried to trash your reputation?"

Deanna swallowed. The question always made her feel uncomfortable. "It's forced me to take a break."

"But you were working on something, right? Can you take that material to another producer? Maybe not right away, but in time. Or even put the music out there yourself?"

"I do have some options," she said. "For now, I'm not stressing about it."

Eric gave her a doubtful look. "You sound casual about everything, but I know that all you've gone through can't have been easy. But what you said is true—you do have other options. Don't let what happened with Brian steal your dream."

Deanna sipped some of the wine. "I know. But it's easier said than done. Though when we were out at A Taste of Soul, it gave me an idea. Even if I don't record another album, I can do small gigs similar to that. There are a lot of opportunities open to me."

Deanna was aware that she sounded almost as though she were trying to convince herself of that fact. But she looked at Eric and hoped that he wasn't getting that sense from her.

"And in reality, the timing isn't even right for me to think about what's next for me with my career," Deanna went on. "With my sisters and I trying to find our mother…" She filled Eric in on the latest, including all of her dead ends in her search. "For all I know, Hart isn't even my mother's real name. I keep praying we'll find her, but there are days I just don't know."

"You'll find her," Eric said, not even the slightest doubt in his tone.

Deanna nodded. Then she was silent as she thought about

all that had happened since the beginning of the year. She'd gone through a myriad of emotions. There had been highs and lows, and she knew the roller coaster ride wasn't over yet.

"So many disappointments," she said softly.

"Hmm?"

"It's just that…" Deanna's voice trailed off, and she exhaled sharply. "I had such high hopes. If nothing else, I expected to have a Christmas song out for the holidays. Something to put my name on to get my career back on track. But most importantly, I really believed my sisters and I would have our mother with us for the holidays this year."

"That can still happen," Eric said with conviction. "And I believe it will. It's not even October yet." He paused briefly. "As for your career, I'm sorry you've had a setback. But I'll tell you what I would tell my students or others going through a dilemma like this. You may have to change your dream to some degree, but you don't have to give it up. Like you said yourself, you could make a nice living singing at venues here in the city. I do know that there were rave reviews about you after you sang at the charity auction."

Now the edges of Deanna's lips curled in a soft smile. "I enjoyed that."

"You have a lot of fans in Cleveland."

"I'm surprised you didn't go into counseling," Deanna said. "You were always so good at getting someone to think about the bright side. To see that whatever problem they were going through was not the end of the world."

"Are you kidding me? I did go into counseling. I may not be an official guidance counselor per se, but I give kids advice every day. In my role as principal, I actually feel I'm able to reach more students. And in a way that doesn't give them a sense of the stigma. For example, they come to me because I'm the principal. If they came to me because I was a guidance counselor, they may feel embarrassed that they had a problem and had to go see someone for special help. This way, they're just talking to the principal, who they can relate to."

"Ah, that makes sense," Deanna said. She paused briefly before saying, "Are you always so accessible to your students the way you were with Risha?"

"Many of my colleagues would say that I should leave the job at school when I go home at the end of the day, but I got into teaching to make a difference. How can I make a difference if I turn a blind eye to problems? So yes, all of the students know that they can come to me with whatever problem they're having, and that I'll be there. That was another thing my ex-wife didn't like about me. She complained that I gave too much of my time to everyone else."

Eric had always been giving with her. It was clearly his nature. But Deanna could see it being a problem for a wife if her husband was always running off to help someone else with an issue.

The next few minutes passed in silence, with both Deanna and Eric finishing off their meals. When Deanna ate the last of her chicken, she placed her hands on her belly and proclaimed, "That was delectable."

"I've got an apple pie in the fridge," Eric said. "I can warm it up."

"Oh, no. I'm stuffed. It's very tempting, but I couldn't possibly eat another bite."

"You sure?"

"Absolutely." Deanna paused. "And I really should be going. But don't worry, I won't eat and run. I'll help you do the dishes."

"You're my guest. I'll take care of the cleanup."

Deanna's phone rang, but like she had done when it had rang earlier in the evening, she stayed put. She was leaving soon enough, and she could check her messages.

"You're not going to get that?" Eric asked.

"I'm one of those people who can ignore a ringing phone. It's something I learned to do when writing my songs. Whoever it is, I'll call them back."

But no sooner had the phone stopped ringing than it began to ring again. "Someone wants to reach you," Eric pointed out.

Deanna went into the adjoining living room and got her purse. As she was able to reach her phone, it stopped ringing and went to voice mail.

Pressing the button on her screen to see her missed calls, her stomach lurched.

"An important call?" Eric asked.

"Uh…" Deanna couldn't believe the number on her screen. "No. Just my sister. I'd better head out. I'll call her from the car."

"I hope everything's all right," Eric commented.

"I'm sure it is. Maybe it's something to do with our mother."

Deanna hoped that Eric couldn't tell she was lying. Because things were far from all right.

Brian, her ex-boyfriend, had just called her two times in a row.

Deanna hoped she made it out of the house before Brian called a third time.

Chapter 9

Thankfully, Brian didn't call again. But once Deanna was a few blocks away, she stopped her car and checked her voice mail.

Brian had left one message, simply saying that he needed to reach her about something important.

Deanna didn't care what he had to say to her—she wasn't going to call him back.

She was glad when the rest of the evening passed without another call from him. And when there were no further calls from him on Friday, Deanna was relieved.

She was definitely feeling a level of anxiety, something she didn't acknowledge until Friday evening when Eric called to reconfirm about Saturday's wedding. She was looking forward to seeing him, more than she expected she would be.

Saturday couldn't come soon enough. Deanna was glad that the wedding wasn't going to be an all-day affair. Eric's friends had opted to have a late-afternoon wedding that would flow right into the evening's reception.

"They're schoolteachers," Eric explained the next day, after the ceremony was over. It had been a small, quaint affair, where the bride had opted for an elegant red dress as opposed to the traditional white. "They were both married before," he went on. "Met each other about six months ago, fell in love quickly and decided there was no point waiting to get married." Eric shrugged. "They definitely look happy."

And they did. Deanna was moved by the way James and Katrina looked at each other as if they were the only two people in the world.

Deanna had seen those very same looks flowing between her sisters and their men. And it was the kind of thing that gave her hope that maybe, just maybe, love could win against all odds.

Having lived in Hollywood, Deanna saw many hookups and breakups. Marriages and disappointments. And her own failed attempts at romance certainly didn't give her hope that she would find her Mr. Right. But being here now, among the happy people celebrating this couple's love, it definitely inspired her.

The wedding party and guests went from the church to the hotel where the reception was being held. Seeing the magically decorated ballroom, Deanna couldn't help feeling a little wistful. This was what she had wanted for herself before she hit thirty. A quaint wedding just like this one, surrounded by the people who mattered the most to her.

"What is it?" Eric asked her, his hand on the small of her back as they headed toward their table.

"Nothing," she lied. Why was she feeling sentimental just because she was at a wedding? If nothing else, it was better that she hadn't gotten married yet, because she had only recently reconnected with her sisters. Now, whenever she tied the knot, they would be with her.

"You want some of that champagne punch?" Eric asked. There was a fountain with the bubbly concoction at the entrance to the reception hall.

"Oh, that sounds nice," Deanna told him.

She took a seat at the table where she and Eric were to be seated. A string quartet was playing a romantic tune, and Deanna enjoyed the music while she waited.

"Deanna?"

At the sound of the female voice, Deanna turned her head. She couldn't have been more surprised to look over her shoulder and see Michelle, the school's secretary.

"Michelle?"

"What are you doing here?"

"Um, Eric asked me to join him." Michelle's eyes widened slightly, and Deanna got the sense that she wasn't happy about what she'd said. "It was a last-minute thing."

"Oh. Eric's here? He didn't mention he was coming."

"He went to get some…" Deanna stopped when she saw him approaching. "Ah, there he is now."

Eric's eyes widened in surprise when he saw Michelle. He greeted her with a peck on the cheek. "Hey, you."

"I didn't know you were going to be here," Michelle said.

Eric shrugged. "I wasn't sure I would be. How is it we're only seeing each other now?"

"My date could only make the reception," she explained. "I didn't want to go to the church on my own." Her eyes moved over both Eric and Deanna with suspicion. "Fancy seeing the both of you here together."

"I needed a date," Eric said. "Deanna graciously agreed to be mine."

"So Deanna was saying," Michelle said. But there was a flicker of something in her eyes. Jealousy? Then she said,

"Too bad I didn't know you were going to this wedding, Eric. We could have been each other's dates."

Eric didn't respond to her comment. Instead he asked, "Where are you sitting?"

"Over there." Michelle pointed to a table on the opposite side of the hall.

"I'll see you a little later, then," he told her.

"Make sure you save me a dance."

Eric sat beside Deanna and took her hand, something that pleased her more than she thought it would. There was something about the way Michelle looked at Eric that made Deanna feel slightly on edge…and she was surprised at the reaction, because she had told herself time and again that she and Eric were just friends.

Was it possible she was actually feeling a smidgen of jealousy?

It was just that Eric looked especially delectable tonight, in a black suit with an off-white shirt. Every time Deanna laid eyes on him, her libido came alive.

"So," Deanna began, and she wasn't sure she even had the right to ask what she was about to, "does Michelle have a crush on you?"

Eric shrugged noncommittally. "We work together."

"Meaning? She can't find you sexy?"

"Do you find me sexy?" Eric asked, turning the tables on her.

Deanna's stomach fluttered at the question. "I think you forget who rejected whom the other night."

"That wasn't…a normal situation. But tonight…"

Eric let his comment trail off, but Deanna knew exactly what he was getting at. And as the evening went on, and he held her in his arms as they danced, she found all the reasons she'd come up with as to why they shouldn't cross that friendship line—now that she wasn't simply looking for an escape from Brian—to be very thin.

She was an adult, and so was he. Why shouldn't they do whatever came naturally?

And perhaps Eric was thinking the same thing, because after the bride and groom thrilled the guests with a big smooch on the dance floor, Eric dipped his head to hers and planted a sweet kiss on her lips.

All the air left Deanna's body in a rush. She wasn't exactly sure what was happening with her, except that Eric turned her on.

"What was that for?" she asked him.

"Just doing something I wish I'd done a long time ago."

Deanna eyed him skeptically. "Are you being serious when you say that? Or now that I'm Deanna Hart, the small-town girl who became a singer…"

Eric stopped moving. He stood with her on the dance floor, looking down at her in surprise. "You're not serious?"

Deanna had regretted the words the moment she'd said them. It was the couple glasses of punch that had made her tongue looser than it should have been. "I'm sorry. I don't know why—"

"If there's any part of you that thinks that, you're completely wrong. I knew you when you were just plain old Deanna, and I liked you then. It's not about who you became."

"I…" Deanna felt like a heel. "I know."

"You don't know how many days I wanted to take you away from Marvin. How many days I wished you would see me as more than just the brother of your boyfriend who you could talk to."

She slipped her arms onto his shoulders and urged his body to move. The love ballad was still playing, and they looked awkward on the floor not dancing.

"Maybe I'm a little jaded," she admitted.

"Excuse me," came the perky female voice, and Deanna was disappointed to see Michelle standing to her left. "Do you mind if I cut in?"

Before Deanna could even respond, Eric was releasing her. He then looked toward Michelle and said, "Sure."

Deanna was left with no choice but to head back to her seat, where she promptly lifted her wineglass and took another sip. What was she doing? Insulting Eric—the one man other than Uncle Dave who had always been decent to her?

Sitting at the table, Deanna watched as Michelle and Eric danced to the rest of the love song, and when the DJ turned it up a notch with a lively hip-hop song, Eric continued to dance with Michelle.

Michelle laughed and talked a lot, but what bothered Deanna was the way she would touch Eric. His arm. His chest. All casually, but it still spoke to Deanna of a sense of familiarity.

And she suddenly wondered if Eric and Michelle had ever been involved on any level before.

Deanna was about to get up and head back toward the dance floor to reclaim Eric when the second song came to an end, but Eric saved her the trouble. He stopped dancing, squeezed Michelle's hand and then started back to the table.

Deanna frowned slightly as he sat beside her, unsure if he was still upset by her thoughtless comment. All she knew was that she needed to explain, to make things right.

"Eric, I'm sorry," Deanna said without preamble. "My comment…it was insensitive and uncalled for. You may even think it shallow." He met her eyes, but his lips were pulled in a tight line. Yeah, he was upset. "It's just—and this is no excuse, because I know you're different—but there have been a lot of men only interested in dating me because of what I do, not who I am."

"I know who you are," Eric said softly. "At least, I thought I did."

"Eric!" Deanna felt a sense of panic. Was he really that upset with her? "Okay, here's a confession. I have a habit of sabotaging things. Maybe I can't trust that things are what they seem, and when they seem too good…I don't know how to handle it. But please, know that I don't really think you would want me only because I became a recording artist. Gosh, I feel like such an idiot for even saying that."

Deanna couldn't have been more surprised when Eric leaned forward and planted his lips on hers. "If that doesn't feel real to you…"

Deanna was speechless. But Eric gave her his classic smile, the one that said everything would be okay. He took her hand and stood. "Dance with me."

Deanna didn't protest. She was just thankful he had forgiven her for being such a snot. And this time when he got her onto the dance floor, even though the music was upbeat, he held her close to him. And soon, his mouth was claiming hers again.

A slow breath oozed out of Deanna when he broke the kiss. In his eyes, she didn't see hesitation like she had Thursday night. She saw white-hot desire.

"Eric…?" Deanna began tentatively. He had rejected her on Thursday, but she was getting a completely different vibe now. She wanted to be sure. "Are we…what are we—?"

"Actually…" Eric said, and taking her by the hand he whizzed her off of the dance floor. He didn't stop walking until he was outside the reception hall in the hotel's foyer area. He took her around a corner, and though Deanna knew she must have been looking up at him with a confused expression, Eric's lips curled in a grin. And when he lowered his mouth onto hers again, good Lord, she was lost.

The sweet touch of his lips against hers elicited the most

wonderful feelings. She was dizzy with desire as he suck-led her bottom lip, then flicked his tongue over it gently, up and down.

And when he broke the kiss this time, Deanna sighed in protest. She had the answer to her question, at least as far as she was concerned. She was ready to act on her feelings of desire for him—and she was pretty certain that he wasn't going to rebuff her this time.

"We're both older now, both past Marvin," Eric said, finally answering her question. "And more importantly, we're both single. Unless you burst my bubble here, it's clear that were both attracted to each other."

"You were the one who burst my bubble the other night," she chastised him, softening the comment with a smile.

"No chance of that happening tonight."

"Oh, really?" Deanna raised an eyebrow. "Who says I'm interested?"

Eric threw his head back and laughed good-naturedly. "Touché." And then, "If you can resist this…"

He kissed her again, his tongue sweeping into her mouth with broad, hot strokes, which left her feeling bedazzled.

Oh, there was no doubt they would end up in his bed…

Something about his touch and his kisses made her feel incredible. Alive.

"I'm ready to leave," Eric said, looking down at her with a heated gaze. "My place?"

"Yes," Deanna rasped.

They went back into the reception hall together, where most of the guests were on the dance floor boogying to an R&B tune. Deanna retrieved her clutch, which she'd placed under the table. Eric said goodbye to the bride and groom and started heading back in her direction. Just as he reached for her hand, she noticed Michelle several feet away, eyeing both of them.

And though Deanna couldn't be sure, it looked to her as though Michelle didn't appear happy.

They were at Eric's place in under twenty minutes. The Trey Martinez CD that Deanna had purchased the first night they'd gone out for dinner was playing in the car, and the romantic tunes were definitely helping to get her in the mood. For the most part, they held hands while Eric drove, listened to the music and didn't speak.

Their bodies—and the desire flowing between them—were speaking for themselves.

And when they got into his house, they continued where they left off, coming together in a frenzy of passion. Even the cat seemed to know not to interrupt them.

Their hands roamed each other's bodies right there in the foyer. Eric had Deanna's body pressed against the front door as his hands smoothed over her belly, then went upward to her exposed cleavage. And then his mouth moved from hers to her jawline, to the underside of her jaw, to her earlobe. His tongue flicked over the lobe, and then he grazed it with his teeth—and Deanna's knees buckled.

"Upstairs," she begged.

Grinning down at her, Eric took her by the hand. Then he led her to the second floor of his home, and to his bedroom. Deanna only registered the warm colors of the room for a nanosecond before Eric swept her into his arms.

"You know what I thought the moment I saw you in this sexy black dress today?" Eric asked her, his hot breath fanning her ear while his hands skimmed the jewel-encrusted fabric at her cleavage.

"What?" Deanna asked.

"How much I wanted to take it off of you."

A rush of heat overwhelmed Deanna. Then Eric was unzipping the back of her dress, pushing the thin straps over her shoulders, letting the slinky black dress fall down her body.

Deanna stepped out of the dress. Eric emitted a low growl when he looked at her in just her bra and panties, and Deanna felt a surge of feminine power.

Eric took her hand and led her to his bed. Her eyes holding his, Deanna lowered herself onto the soft comforter. Eric cradled her face with his palm, and Deanna was struck by just how different he was from other men. He was sensitive and strong in a way that other men she'd dated weren't.

Her raw sexual need for Eric increased as he shed his tuxedo blazer and then took his time undoing his shirt. Deanna watched him, mesmerized. With each button that was undone, more of his sexy chest was revealed. His golden-brown chest was muscular, and his abs...they were as well defined as any athlete who spent hours honing his body to perfection.

"I didn't know you were hiding all that under your clothes," Deanna said, reaching out to help pull the shirt off of his body. Then she placed both palms on his warm skin.

"Wait a second," Eric said to her.

Eric turned and crossed the room, and she soon saw what he was doing. He had a stereo system in the room, and he turned it on. Moments later, the smooth sounds of Brian Mc-Knight filled the air.

As he walked back toward her, he was unbuttoning his pants. Then he let them fall to the floor and kicked them off. All that remained on his magnificent body was a pair of white Jockey underwear.

Deanna shuddered as she reveled in the sight of his erection straining against the cotton fabric. He was large and hard, and she couldn't wait to make love to him.

"Wow," was all Deanna could manage to say.

A ragged breath escaped Eric's lips, and stepping forward he slipped his fingers into her short hair. "Do you know how sexy you look? Wearing only your bra and panties and those incredible shoes?"

Deanna had taken extra time to decide what to wear today, and the black lacy bra and panty set was her favorite. And she knew that Eric would love the four-inch heels with criss-crossing straps and a heart-shaped jewel over the middle of her foot.

Her efforts had been entirely worth it, simply for the look in Eric's eyes as he regarded her.

He lowered himself onto the bed beside her and immediately began to kiss her. As he did, he urged her onto her back and traced the delicate material of her bra with his fingertips. Deanna sucked in a quick breath as the light touch of his fingers caused heat to flood through her. She wanted him so badly, and she knew that she would go crazy if he didn't start touching her erogenous zones soon.

She arched her back, inviting Eric to taste her breasts. Breaking the kiss, he smiled at her as he undid the front clasp of her bra and let it fall open, freeing her breasts. Her nipples were already tingling with raw sexual fervor.

Eric's face was ripe with passion as his eyes moved hungrily over her breasts. And then he brought his mouth down onto one of the taut peaks, running his lips across it before he parted them and took her nipple into his mouth. He tweaked her other nipple into a solid peak, all the while teasing her nipple in his mouth with flicks of his tongue and gentle suckles.

"Oh, Eric…" He suckled her harder, driving Deanna mad with lust. "I need…I want…"

Her voice trailed off on a rapturous sigh as his mouth moved to her other breast. The feelings assailing her were absolutely amazing, but when Eric brought a hand between her legs and stroked her center through her panties, she erupted in flames.

"You're beautiful, baby." His fingers slipped under the

fabric, and Deanna moaned in pleasure. He stroked her sensitive flesh, and it was as though she were experiencing this kind of sexual pleasure for the first time. Had anything ever felt this incredible?

She gripped the bedsheets, allowing herself to enjoy the pleasure he was giving. His mouth moved from her nipple, over her breast, to the hollow between both mounds, then to the other nipple. All the while he stroked her, bringing her to the edge of bliss.

He broke contact with her only to ease his body over hers, and even that small moment of time with him not touching her was too much. She needed him. Touching her. Kissing her. Inside of her.

Eric stripped off her panties, and Deanna heard a grumbling sound emanate from his chest. She could see his impressive shaft and knew how much he wanted her.

"Make love to me," Deanna begged.

"Oh, I will," Eric said, the soft words a promise.

And just when Deanna thought for sure that he was going to settle between her thighs, he instead brought his mouth down onto her belly. He kissed a path over her abdomen, making her even more heady with desire.

He kissed her skin, nibbled, teased it with flicks of his tongue. All the while his fingers stroked and tantalized.

"That's it, baby," he said as she moaned in pleasure. "Right now, it's all about you."

Those were words he meant. Because he took his time with her, used his fingers and his mouth and—oh, goodness—his tongue to elicit the most wonderful feelings. And soon, Deanna was falling over the edge.

"That's it," Eric said softly. "I've got you, baby."

"Eric…" Deanna slipped an arm around his neck and urged him upward. "I need you inside of me." She sought out his lips and kissed him hungrily.

And as they kissed, that was when Eric slid into her. And if Deanna thought that what she'd felt before was amazing—it was nothing compared to the sensation that now came over her.

"Oh, baby," she whispered, her voice hoarse with sexual longing. "You feel so good."

Eric moaned in response to her words and began to pick up his pace. His strokes were slow and deep, but as Deanna wrapped her arms tightly around his waist, he began to move faster.

"You're driving me crazy," Deanna told him, snaking her leg around his, moving it up and down as she jutted her hips upward. Bending his head, Eric hungrily took her other nipple in his mouth and sucked with such fervor that Deanna thought she might orgasm again.

"Oh, God, Eric…"

"Yes, baby," he rasped.

And then, filling her with a blinding thrust, he kissed her. His tongue went deep in her mouth, matching how deep his shaft was inside of her. And there was something about the deep and tender way he was kissing her and moving inside of her that was like nothing else Deanna had ever experienced. And suddenly, she was gripping the sheets with her hands and closing her eyes as she succumbed to the sweetest pleasure.

She dug her fingers into his back, holding on for the ride. Eric's thrusts became faster, more urgent. And soon his body was tensing and he was joining her in that magical place.

The sounds of their heavy breathing mixed with the sounds of Brian McKnight singing about crazy love. And surprisingly, Deanna found that she was moved by the lyrics. Almost as though what she and Eric had done was beyond simply sex.

No, she told herself, *it's just the mood the music is creating.* That and the fact that sex with Eric had been far more spectacular than with any other man. And yes, when she thought about it, it was a little bit crazy that she was here in bed with her former friend, and he had just rocked her world.

He had taken his time with her, completely pleasing her before he worried about pleasing himself.

Eric then kissed her—and Deanna stopped thinking.

Crazy or not, she was enjoying every moment with him.

Chapter 10

"Hey, you," Deanna said as she planted a kiss on Eric's cheek the next morning. He had just opened his eyes, but she had been awake for at least ten minutes, her mind replaying every wonderful moment of the previous night. Now that he was awake, she was ready for round four.

Or was it five? She'd lost count.

"Hey, yourself," Eric said. He trailed a finger along her cheek. "What time is it?"

Deanna glanced over her shoulder at the bedside digital clock. "Seven-fourteen."

"Sheesh." Eric groaned. "I should still be sleeping. We should still be sleeping. Since we didn't do much of that in this bed."

"Are you complaining?" Deanna gave him another kiss, this time on his lips, nice and slow as if to wake him into a state of arousal.

"No. Definitely not complaining."

"Good. Because I'm ready for more."

Eric's eyebrows shot up. "You are?"

"That was some good loving," Deanna said, then she buried her face in his shoulder and giggled.

Eric's hand slid down her naked back and rested on her behind. "Mmm. Suddenly, I'm not feeling so tired."

Deanna lifted her head. "No?"

He pulled her body on top of his. "Uh-uh."

"Oh." Then his hand covered her breast as his mouth found hers, and that was all it took. "Ohhh…"

A few hours later, Deanna was dressed in one of Eric's T-shirts, which hung to her midthigh, and she was watching him as he doled out her portion of the scrambled eggs. Sadie, who had protested loudly outside of his bedroom that she was hungry, had finished her breakfast and was now grooming herself.

"Seriously, Eric, at least let me get the coffee."

"Sit," he told her, placing a plate of eggs and toast in front of her. Then he poured her a cup of coffee and also set it on the table.

The least Deanna could do was wait for him, so she didn't start eating until he had his own toast, eggs and coffee ready.

Eric was smiling at her as he sat across from her at the kitchen table. It was the kind of smile that made Deanna blush, because she was pretty sure he was remembering a part of their scorching night.

"Last month, if anyone told me that you'd be sitting at my table wearing only my shirt, I would have told them that they'd lost their mind."

"Tell me about it," Deanna concurred.

Eric ate a bite of his toast, then asked, "Regrets?"

"Are you kidding me? It was an amazing night." She shrugged. "Though a bit unexpected."

KIMANI ROMANCE

An Important Message from the Publisher

Dear Reader,

Because you've chosen to read one of our fine novels, I'd like to say "thank you"! And, as a special way to say thank you, I'm offering to send you two more Kimani™ Romance novels and two surprise gifts—absolutely FREE! These books will keep it real with true-to-life African American characters that turn up the heat and sizzle with passion.

Please enjoy the free books and gifts with our compliments...

Glenda Howard
For Kimani Press™

FREE GIFT SEAL
EDITOR'S THANK YOU

Peel off Seal and
Place Inside...

W e'd like to send you two free books to introduce you to Kimani™ Romance books. These novels feature strong, sexy women, and African-American heroes that are charming, loving and true. Our authors fill each page with exceptional dialogue, exciting plot twists, and enough sizzling romance to keep you riveted until the very end!

KIMANI ROMANCE...LOVE'S ULTIMATE DESTINATION

Your two books have combined cover price of $12.50 in the U.S. o $14.50 in Canada, but are yours **FREE!**

We'll even send you two wonderful surprise gifts. You can't lose!

THE EDITOR'S "THANK YOU" FREE GIFTS INCLUDE:

Two Kimani™ Romance Novels
Two exciting surprise gifts

YES! I have placed my Editor's "thank you" Free Gifts seal in the space provided at right. Please send me 2 FREE Books, and my 2 FREE Mystery Gifts. I understand that I am under no obligation to purchase anything further, as explained on the back of this card.

PLACE FREE GIFTS SEAL HERE

168/368 XDL FTF5

Please Print

FIRST NAME

LAST NAME

ADDRESS

APT.#   CITY

STATE/PROV.   ZIP/POSTAL CODE

Thank You!

The Reader Service - Here's How It Works:

Accepting your 2 free books and 2 free gifts (gifts valued at approximately $10.00) places you under no obligation to buy anything. You may keep the books and gifts and return the shipping statement marked "cancel." If you do not cancel, about a month later we'll send you 4 additional books and bill you just $4.94 each in the U.S. or $5.49 each in Canada. That is a savings of at least 21% off the cover price. Shipping and handling is just 50¢ per book in the U.S. and 75¢ per book in Canada.* You may cancel at any time, but if you choose to continue, every month we'll send you 4 more books, which you may either purchase at the discount price or return to us and cancel your subscription.
*Terms and prices subject to change without notice. Prices do not include applicable taxes. Sales tax applicable in N.Y. Canadian residents will be charged applicable taxes. Offer not valid in Quebec. All orders subject to credit approval. Credit or debit balances in a customer's account(s) may be offset by any other outstanding balance owed by or to the customer. Offer available while quantities last. Books received may not be as shown. Please allow 4 to 6 weeks for delivery.

If offer card is missing write to: The Reader Service, P.O. Box 1867, Buffalo, NY 14240-1867 or visit www.ReaderService.com

BUSINESS REPLY MAIL
FIRST-CLASS MAIL   PERMIT NO. 717   BUFFALO, NY

POSTAGE WILL BE PAID BY ADDRESSEE

THE READER SERVICE
PO BOX 1867
BUFFALO NY 14240-9952

NO POSTAGE
NECESSARY
IF MAILED
IN THE
UNITED STATES

"You think so?" Eric asked.

Deanna bulged her eyes. "You don't?"

Eric ate a morsel of egg before speaking. "I guess that depends on your perspective. I already told you, I was always interested in you."

Deanna said nothing as she took her time chewing her toast. She wasn't exactly sure what to say. Because she didn't know what Eric's expectations were in terms of moving forward.

"Maybe, as much as you were into Marvin, there was a part of you that was attracted to me," Eric said tentatively. "Maybe that's why we were both so strongly attracted to each other now, when we met again."

Deanna half nodded, half shrugged. "Maybe." And for some reason, she felt compelled to add, "I really suck at relationships, Eric."

"You've never had a relationship with me."

So her instincts weren't off. He was thinking beyond being involved physically. "No, but there have been others. Other perfectly nice men whom it didn't work out with. And I can't blame them. There's something about me and relationships."

"Like I said, you've never had a relationship with me." And again, he offered her one of his sexy smiles.

"Seriously, Eric—last night was great, but I don't know about tomorrow." Though she knew that she wouldn't soon tire of being in his arms.

"We don't have to think about tomorrow," he said. "Just take things a day at a time."

Deanna's stomach twisted. She was feeling anxious, and she didn't know why.

Yes, she knew why. She was back to thinking about the fact that she didn't want to lose Eric as a friend. They'd fallen into bed together, something she'd done because she knew him well and trusted him. But she didn't want him getting his hopes up.

"Maybe it has to do with my past," she said. "Never knowing my father, my mother leaving." She shrugged. "I think there's a part of me that inherently doesn't trust when things are going okay. I'm always waiting for the other shoe to drop."

Eric scooted his chair around the table so that he was sitting beside her. And then he took her hand. "There's no doubt that stuff has an effect on a person. But half the battle is knowing what your issues are. There's no reason for your past to hold you back."

"I know," Deanna said, but she was thinking that it wasn't so easy. "I like you, Eric. I really do. I always have. And, it's obvious there is an attraction between us. But it's also obvious to me that many people have screwed up good friendships because they've gotten involved romantically."

"That doesn't have to—"

"Let me finish," Deanna said. "We're both adults. And there's no denying the chemistry between us. It led to a fantastic night," she added with a smile. "I wouldn't mind more nights like that...but in a no-strings-attached sort of way."

Eric was silent as he regarded her. Then he said, "No strings attached?"

"We're attracted to each other. Maybe that's all it is, maybe there's more. I'm not sure that we have to label it. I've seen people label their relationships too quickly and it leads to problems." When Eric said nothing, she continued. "For one thing, I'm working at the school now. If things go sour..." Deanna sighed softly. "What I'm saying is, I like how I feel when I'm with you. I trust you. I always did. So maybe it's okay if we have a relationship where we...enjoy each other... but with no expectations."

"Friends with benefits?" Eric supplied.

"I guess if there's a label for it, that would be it. Friends with benefits. For one thing, I don't know how long I'm going to be here, or when I'm heading back to Hollywood. And you may be moving to Cincinnati in the near future. And then there's the search for my mother, which is taking up a lot of my time and effort. Let's just not complicate things by expecting more. Friends with benefits works for me." She raised an eyebrow as she held his gaze. "Does it work for you?"

Hours later, Eric was at the gym and thinking about Deanna, somewhat perplexed by the turn of events after what had been an incredible night.

Friends with benefits works for me. Does it work for you?

The short answer: heck, yes. He wasn't about to turn down the opportunity to spend time with her—to feel her naked body against his as he had last night. But he still felt somewhat unsettled about the way she had set out the terms of their involvement. He had been on a high, having felt that they'd connected emotionally as well as sexually. He had figured that she'd been on a high, as well—until her almost dispassionate talk about how they should be friends with benefits.

Her demeanor at the breakfast table had been a stark contrast to how she had behaved in his bed last night. He had felt the way her body had melted against his. He had tasted the sweet little sighs coming from her mouth.

Eric turned up the speed of the treadmill so that he was at a full-on run. He didn't want a friends-with-benefits relationship with Deanna. She was the one woman with whom he thought he could have it all.

She wasn't the only one with demons. He had his own. And he was well aware that his might complicate a relationship.

What he hoped was that with the right woman, they could overcome their hurdles together.

And he wanted Deanna to be that woman.

* * *

Later that evening, Deanna was at Uncle Dave's and thinking about Eric. She felt a smidgen of guilt, wondering if she'd hurt him.

Because the truth was, they'd shared a remarkable night—and for her to talk about being friends with benefits the morning after must have diminished, at least in his mind, the experience.

That hadn't been her plan. It was just the way he'd been looking at her, so full of hope…and Deanna had been assailed with doubt.

The idea of losing Eric as a friend was almost too impossible to bear…especially now that they'd reconnected.

They'd fallen into bed, something that seemed bound to happen, given the sparks that had been flying between them the first moment she'd laid eyes on him again. She definitely wanted more of that, but she feared that trying to define their relationship would lead to the end of it.

Maybe it was the influence of Brian. How badly things had ended. She knew Eric wasn't Brian, but still…

Deanna pulled her knees to her chest as she sat on the bed and inhaled a deep breath. She held it before releasing it slowly.

"You really are anxious about relationships," she said softly. And for some reason, she felt especially anxious about this one not working.

Eric was saying all the right things, and he definitely seemed to care. But he wouldn't be the first person who cared about her to disappoint her.

Her mother had done that when she was seven years old.

Deanna's phone rang, and she quickly crawled across the bed to the night table to retrieve it. She was hoping it was Eric, who hadn't called since she'd left his place.

But when she saw the number displayed on her screen, Deanna's heart almost exploded in her chest.

Brian!

She quickly hit the button to reject the call. Her stomach was suddenly feeling queasy. She didn't like this, not one bit. Why was Brian suddenly trying so hard to reach out to her?

It didn't take more than a minute before the phone rang again.

She didn't answer.

But then the phone rang a third time, and Deanna felt the nightmare starting once more.

There was only one way to deal with this, and that was to nip the problem in the bud. So she answered the call.

"Yes?" she said tersely.

"Baby." Brian sounded both delighted and relieved.

"I'm not your baby."

"Come on—is that how you're going to treat your old boyfriend?"

"What do you want?" she snapped.

"I've missed you."

This was why he was calling her? "I'm not having this conversation with you," Deanna told him. "Hell, how many months have we been broken up?"

"And each day it gets harder without you."

"Goodb—"

"I want us to work together again," Brian quickly said. "I've spoken with Steven from the record label, and he still wants to release your next album."

For a moment, Deanna was stunned. This was what she'd wanted to hear for so long.

And yet, she no longer wanted it if Brian were attached to the deal.

"I'm not even in town," Deanna said, though she owed him no explanation.

"Well, when you get back, we can get started on the tracks again. I think Miss You is solid. And…and we can work on repairing our relationship."

"We have no relationship."

And then Brian snapped. "This is what you do. You get involved with someone, and for a few weeks it's good. Then you start acting like you're being smothered. I'm sorry about what I did, but you never even gave us a fair chance."

"Goodbye," she said and quickly hung up.

As she drew in deep breaths, she realized that her hands were shaking.

Brian shouldn't be getting to her, not at this point in her life. But his words had.

Then you start acting like you're being smothered…

That struck a chord with her. And as much as she wished Brian was just spewing hurtful words, she knew that he was right on the mark with that comment.

And maybe that explained why she was so concerned about her and Eric getting involved.

Because there was something about her that always led to her pushing men away.

Even the good ones.

Wednesday afternoon, Deanna went to the school for the rehearsal of *Annie* as scheduled. For the past few days, ever since Brian's call, she'd felt anxious.

His words had truly gotten to her, made her take a good, hard look at herself.

Eric had called her a couple of times, but she hadn't responded. In part because of what Brian had said, she wanted more than ever to drive home the idea that she and Eric were friends with benefits. Which meant they didn't have to talk every day.

There were no expectations.

She didn't go to the office to see Eric, instead heading straight to the auditorium. She was running a few minutes late, and by the looks of it, everyone was there. As she strolled down to the group of students, Mr. Singh and Mrs. Olney, she could feel the tension in the room.

A group of girls was standing together on stage, giggling. They were simply doing what kids normally did—being silly if they had a moment of spare time. But Mr. Singh approached them and angrily said, "Are you ready? Or are you going to goof off the entire time you're here?"

The girls stopped their snickering, frowns instantly taking shape on their faces.

"Good," Mr. Singh said.

"Sorry I'm late," Deanna said, taking the stairs on the stage. Not for the first time she wondered why this man was involved in directing a group of eighth-grade students in a theatrical production. He seemed to have no patience for them.

His lips were tight as he shot a gaze in her direction, and his "Hello" was definitely flat.

"Good afternoon, everyone," Deanna said, stepping to the center of the stage. "As I said I'd do last time, I've prepared some vocal exercises we can start with. If Mr. Singh agrees, maybe we can separate into two groups. One group will be with me and Mrs. Olney to do the vocal exercises, while the other group can be with Mr. Singh to rehearse lines. How does that sound?"

"Yeahs" were spoken all around her.

Deanna darted a glance at Mr. Singh, worried that he would disagree or feel that she was stepping on his toes. But he said nothing.

"Okay, then. Let's do that. Why don't I take this half of the room?" She gestured with her hands and indicated those closest to her. "The rest of you can go with Mr. Singh." She smiled cheerfully, hoping that that smile would affect everybody's mood in a positive way.

Keith was in her group and pushed his way to the front. "Can I sing my part for you?" he asked. "I already know it."

"Actually," Deanna began, "everyone will do the vocal warm-up together. Everybody follow me. I'll sing one line, then you repeat the line. Okay?"

The kids nodded.

"Fa la la la la," Deanna sang, then paused. Once the kids repeated her line, she continued, changing the length, tone and tempo of the simple words.

Then she took the next group of students, and ten minutes later Mr. Singh asked that the chorus practice one of the songs that he'd sent them home to learn.

Deanna watched, impressed. Since the last time she'd been here, these girls seemed to have gotten more comfortable with their roles, and their voices were stronger. As they sang, some swayed their shoulders in time with the beat or clapped their hands, allowing their bodies to feel the music, as well. It was the kind of rendition that Deanna knew parents would be proudly recording and capturing with cameras. And she knew that with further rehearsals, the kids would only get better and better.

An hour later, everyone seemed happy with what had undoubtedly been a productive rehearsal. Mr. Singh said he was pleased, but he didn't look it.

And Deanna found herself wondering if he was displeased with her.

So she approached him after the kids had left and said, "Can I talk to you for a moment?"

Again, his lips were set in a tight line as he faced her. "Sure."

"Is there something I've done that upset you?" she asked, getting right to the issue.

"Why would you ask that?" Mr. Singh asked, but he didn't meet her eyes.

"Honestly, you don't seem too happy to have me here. I've given it thought on a few occasions so I could see if maybe I was imagining things, and I don't think I am. If you really don't want me working on this production, then just say so. I get that it's your baby, and I'll respect your decision if you tell me that you'd rather not have me be a part of it. But I'm enjoying working on this production, and I think the kids are enjoying having me around."

Mr. Singh sank down onto the one of the auditorium seats. "I'm sorry if I've given you that impression. I didn't mean to make you feel uncomfortable."

Deanna sensed that there was more he wanted to say, so she didn't speak, just nodded her head.

"It's not that I don't want you here," he went on. "It's that… there's a lot going on in my life. It's my wife."

Deanna didn't know what she'd expected, but she hadn't expected him to mention a wife. "Your wife? Is she okay?"

"She left me. In the summer. After twenty years of marriage. Our teenage daughter left for college, and you see, that was what she was waiting for. She told me that she didn't want to leave while Sarita was still under our roof. The problem is, I had no idea she wanted to leave at all. I…" He swallowed. "I haven't been the same since."

"Oh, my goodness. I'm so sorry."

Mr. Singh shrugged. "I keep hoping every day that she'll come back. But she hardly wants to talk to me. All she'll say is that she put up with me for years. I know I haven't always been the easiest man to get along with, and I suppose now it's only worse for those around me. I've been lost in my own world."

Deanna took a seat beside him. "Well, that's understandable."

"You love somebody for so long, you think that they love you back. You think that you'll always be together. And then suddenly…suddenly they tell you it's over."

"Mr. Singh—"

"Sanjay, please."

"Sanjay," Deanna said and offered him a little smile. "No wonder you're unhappy. I'm so sorry you're going through this."

He swallowed with difficulty and then he stood. "I shouldn't burden you with my problems."

"It's no problem," Deanna said. "I'm happy to listen."

"I…I bought one of your CDs. I listened closely to the words in your love songs. And I thought…maybe you'd have some advice?"

If he only knew. Just because Deanna sang about love didn't mean she had it all together in the romance department.

But she was touched that he'd bought one of her CDs. It told her that he regretted his unflattering comment the first time they'd met.

"Just be honest," Deanna told him. "Tell her how you feel. Tell her that you miss her. And ask her what you need to do to help make things better."

Mr. Singh nodded, his expression saying he was receptive to her advice. Though Deanna felt a little weird giving it.

"Twenty years," he reiterated. "How does twenty years come to an end so suddenly?"

At the sound of footsteps, Deanna looked over her shoulder. Eric was approaching. Even as her stomach lurched, she thought about Mr. Singh's question—how twenty years could come to an end so suddenly.

That was precisely what Deanna wanted to avoid. The kind of heartbreak that came when a relationship of that magnitude ended. No wonder Mr. Singh was always in a foul mood.

Eric smiled as he reached them, but the smile didn't reach

his eyes. "Hey, Sanjay," he said casually. Then, looking at Deanna, he simply said her name. "Deanna."

"Hi." Deanna's voice was faint.

"Can I talk to you for a minute?" Eric asked her. "In my office?"

"Yeah, sure."

And as Deanna followed Eric out of the auditorium, she got the distinct impression that this trip to the principal's office wasn't going to be a pleasant one.

Because she knew exactly what Eric wanted to talk to her about.

Chapter 11

Deanna followed Eric into the school office, where she saw Michelle gathering her belongings, clearly ready to leave for the day. Her eyes volleyed from Deanna to Eric, and Deanna would bet her last dollar that a look of unease passed over Michelle's face.

"Hey, Michelle," Deanna said, offering her a smile.

"Hi." Unlike the first time they'd met, Michelle's smile seemed forced. The only thing that had changed between then and now was that she was certain Michelle suspected there was more going on between her and Eric than merely a friendship. Which only confirmed Deanna's suspicion that the secretary had a major crush on the principal.

"See you tomorrow, Eric," Michelle said, her tone and smile brighter now that she was speaking to him.

Whatever, Deanna thought.

"Evening, Michelle," Eric told her. Then he opened the door to his office and gestured for Deanna to enter.

Once she stepped inside, Eric closed the door. A beat passed before he leveled a confused look on her.

Deanna spoke before he could. "How's Risha?"

She saw something pass in Eric's eyes, almost a hint of humor. He knew she had brought up Risha as a way to delay the real conversation he wanted to have with her.

But he replied nonetheless. "She's tough. A strong kid. So overall, she's doing well. She's here and she's smiling, but I know that emotionally she's in a tough place."

"You said that the police tracked down her father." Eric had told her that at the wedding. "Is he still in jail?"

Eric shook his head. "Unfortunately not. He's been released on bail, with strict instructions to stay away from his wife and daughter. But unfortunately that doesn't mean a thing."

"Ain't that the truth."

"So far, there haven't been any problems. Hopefully it stays that way." In an instant, Eric's expression changed. His eyes narrowed on Deanna. "Enough about Risha. What's going on with you?"

"Nothing."

A slight frown marred his face. "You're going to pretend you don't know what I'm talking about?"

Another beat passed, then Deanna released a harried breath. "I know…you're upset that I didn't return your calls. It's not that I'm ignoring you. I've just been…preoccupied." She knew that her words sounded lame, but they were true. She had been making more calls in an attempt to locate her mother. "Sorry."

"Sorry?"

"That's all I can say."

Eric pursed his lips as he eyed her. Then he said in a low voice, "One minute we're rocking each other's worlds. The next, I'm not hearing from you."

It didn't make sense, but Deanna had been racked with confusing feelings after leaving Eric's bed. Their connection had been easy, and she should be feeling elated. But on the contrary, she was more uneasy than ever.

"So tell me the truth," Eric said. "Why didn't you return my calls?"

Because I'm afraid of getting hurt, was the thought that popped into Deanna's mind. But she said, "I already told you."

One of Eric's eyebrows shot up, the look on his face one of pure skepticism. Then he took a few steps forward, leaned in close and said, "I don't believe you."

Eric's warm breath was fanning her cheek, causing a tingling sensation to spread over Deanna's body.

Next, he placed his hands on her upper arms. "The thing is, I was annoyed with you," he said. "And I was prepared to stay that way. And then I set my eyes on you...and all I can think about is taking you back to my bed."

Now, a delicious rush coursed through her.

"What exactly are you afraid of?" Eric asked her. "That we won't be good together?"

"Oh, I know we'll be good together. Aquarius and Libra have a great connection—mentally and sexually." She had checked it out, out of curiosity.

"You needed to turn to astrology to figure out if we'd be good together?" Eric asked, now trailing a finger along her cheek. "You couldn't figure that out from the time we spent together?"

Maybe it was his husky voice, and the way he was touching her, but Deanna was finding it hard to think. In fact, she didn't really care about talking. All she wanted to do was get naked.

"Friends with benefits," she managed.

"Oh, we would both most definitely benefit from another romp in my bedroom."

Deanna felt a zap of heat at the core of her womanhood.

And when Eric flicked his tongue over her earlobe, that was it. She knew she couldn't resist him anymore.

"You have anywhere to be?" she asked. Then, wanting to dole out some teasing of her own, she placed her hand on his groin and felt his erection.

"My place," Eric said hotly. "Now."

"Let's go."

The moment they got to his house, Eric took Deanna's hand and led her up the stairs. Sadie mewled for some attention, but he gave her only a quick pat on the head before continuing on with Deanna to his bedroom.

For years, he had dreamed about being with her intimately, imagined how incredible it would be.

The real thing far exceeded his imagination.

Their sexual connection was explosive. They made love with the kind of ease that said they'd been together a thousand times before.

Sadie followed them into the bedroom, but Eric scooped up the cat and put her out the door. He didn't need her to witness what he and Deanna were about to do.

By the time he turned from closing the door, Deanna was throwing her arms around his neck. The force of her body sent him backward against the door. And when her lips pressed against his, Eric's body erupted in flames.

Instantly, he was hard. He had the kind of fiery connection with Deanna that he knew he would never bore of.

She was the aggressor, using her tongue to force his lips apart. She kissed him with fervor, her tongue twisting with his. And all the while she made these soft little purring sounds that drove Eric wild.

Deanna moved her mouth to his neck, where she pressed her soft lips against his skin. A peck here, a peck there. She linked fingers with his and pushed his hands up so that they were against the door.

Oh, yeah, she was taking charge. And Eric was loving every minute of her boldness.

Easing her head back, she looked up at him and smiled slyly. Then she let go of his hands and stepped backward. Her eyes locked on his, and her fingers went to the top button of her blouse. Slowly, she undid it.

Eric's heart was beating a mile a minute as he watched her. One button undone, now another. And when she undid the third, her cleavage came into view. Two ample mounds pushed together in her red lacy bra.

"Damn," he uttered, taking a step toward her.

"No," Deanna told him. "You stay right there. You're only allowed to watch."

Eric growled. He was so turned on, his entire body was throbbing with need.

Finally, Deanna got the blouse off. She tossed it to the floor. Then she went to work on her jeans, her lips curling as she began to push them down her hips. He couldn't imagine what his face looked like, but she was clearly taking pleasure in knowing that she was torturing him.

The jeans were tight, and she had to wrestle with them to get them off. Then she threw them, as though happy to be rid of the uncooperative garment.

And then she stood in front of him with her lacy red bra and matching panties.

Eric's breath caught in his chest. Deanna was a vision of loveliness. Those large breasts and curved hips…she had the kind of hourglass figure that made men go wild.

"I need to touch you," Eric growled.

"Not yet," Deanna told him. And then she swayed her body, as though dancing to a slow and seductive beat. Her hands went to her large breasts, which she delicately touched with the tips of her fingers, as though in invitation. She had to know that she was driving him crazy.

She continued to sway, now moving slowly downward as one hand went to her abdomen. She gyrated in the most seductive manner until she was back to a standing position.

Eric had to force himself to swallow.

Grinning at him, she reached behind her body to unclasp her bra…and then her breasts fell free.

"Deanna," Eric uttered, taking in the sight of her erect nipples. "You're stunning."

She made another purring sound, and Eric wanted nothing more than to take her in his arms and drive his shaft into her. But he let her continue.

Her hands now moved to her panties, which she slowly pulled down her hips and then kicked off of her body.

She was perfect. Absolutely gorgeous.

"I need to have you," he told her, advancing. He couldn't wait any longer.

But Deanna jumped backward before he could reach her and started to saunter quickly toward his bed. She giggled, no doubt in response to what must have been a look of surprise on his face.

"Oh, that's how you want it?"

Eric lunged forward, but Deanna jumped onto the bed. She giggled again as she vaulted to the other side in an effort to escape him. But Eric moved quickly, ensnaring her ankle with his hand. And though she tried to flail, he was too strong for her, easily pulling her body back to his side of the bed.

He had a view of her backside, and he squeezed it with both of his hands. No longer fighting, Deanna moaned. Eric did the same as he came down onto the bed beside her and eased her onto her back. The moment her breasts came into view, he took a nipple into his mouth.

"Oh, baby," Deanna rasped as he suckled her.

He went to the other nipple, teasing her even more. He had been at her mercy before, but now she was at his.

"I need…I need you inside of me."

"This is what you get," Eric told her, tweaking both of her nipples now. "The same kind of sexual torture you just gave to me."

She moaned and arched her back. He suckled her again as he smoothed one hand down the length of her perfect body, knowing that as much as he was torturing her, he was also torturing himself.

Because he needed to be inside of her.

"I can't take it," she whimpered.

And neither could he. So he stood and quickly stripped out of his clothes as he watched her chest rise and fall quickly. How had any man not snatched her up and made her his by now?

Eric wasn't about to complain. Because he wanted no other man to have her.

And as he went onto the bed and pulled her on top of him and guided his shaft into her, all he could think was that this was meant to be.

That she was finally his.

Chapter 12

For the next couple of weeks, Deanna and Eric fell into a routine. She came to school to help with rehearsals—and then she left with him to go back to his place and make spectacular love. She also spent time with him on the weekends, enjoying their carnal lust for each other.

There was no doubt that Eric was the best lover she'd ever been with. He was attentive and fun and had stamina. She couldn't want for anything more when it came to the sexual connection between them.

Which didn't surprise her. Deanna didn't anticipate ever getting tired of being with him.

She and Eric were going with the flow, for which she was grateful. Because she knew that labeling their relationship would only cause her anxiety.

"You're spending an awful lot of time with Eric," Callie said to her when Deanna and her sisters were out for dinner on a Thursday evening. Now that Callie was working as a guidance counselor at a school in East Cleveland and making wedding plans, they didn't get to see all that much of each other. And Natalie was doing a lot of traveling with Michael to away games. They'd quickly taken advantage of the opportunity to get together to catch up on how Callie's wedding plans were coming along as well as to catch up on each other's lives.

"Yeah," Deanna said. "It's been nice."

"Nice," Natalie said with a chuckle, lightly punching Deanna on the shoulder. "That look on your face says you two are raising the roof!"

"Someone's got to give you two some competition," Deanna retorted, and the three of them laughed.

When the laughter subsided, Callie said, "Seriously, though, are you two getting serious?"

"Yeah," Natalie concurred. "That's what we want to know."

"We're…we're having fun," Deanna answered.

Natalie frowned. "I'm sure Eric wants more than just fun with you. You two spent a lot of time together when we were younger. I remember him coming by to pick you up, take you to the movies, whatever."

"Yeah, every time Marvin upset me, I'd call him."

"And me," Natalie added sadly. "When I upset you. I played a big part in hurting you, too."

Deanna shrugged. She didn't care about the past anymore, not at all. "None of that matters, remember?" When Natalie emitted a little sigh, Deanna said, "It's as though you expect me to go back to being mad at you, even though we've moved on."

"I guess I just can't believe how far we've come," Natalie said. "In a way, I keep waiting for the other shoe to drop."

Deanna's eyes widened at the comment. Those had been the exact words she'd used with Eric.

"Anyway," Natalie continued, "I'm glad Eric's still there for you like he was back then."

"Me, too." That much Deanna could agree with, no matter if she still wasn't willing to look beyond today. "He's taking me to his cabin this weekend."

"Oooh, sounds fun," Natalie said, winking.

"It was his birthday yesterday," Deanna explained. "So he wants us to spend the weekend together."

"Sounds serious," Callie chimed.

"We're enjoying each other," Deanna repeated herself.

"From everything you've said," Callie began, "Eric has always been there for you. I think he could be the one."

"You're determined to see me settle down, aren't you?" Deanna asked.

"What I don't want to see is you run from someone who's great for you," Callie said.

"I'm not running," Deanna replied.

"No, but you're also making sure to say that your relationship is only casual. I don't want to see you push Eric away."

Deanna waved a dismissive hand. "Eric and I have an agreement."

"Agreement?" Callie's lips twisted and she shook her head. "You can't make agreements when it comes to love."

Deanna chuckled mirthlessly. "I don't know why you're so hell-bent on talking about love."

"Because we know exactly what you're doing," Natalie pitched in. "You don't trust love, you don't want to get hurt—we get it. But you can put all the walls up around your heart that you want to, it's not going to protect you from falling in love."

"Wow, listen to you two," Deanna said, brushing off the comment. "From cynical to sentimental. I'm impressed."

Callie frowned. "We're serious. I know all about putting guards up—and look what it cost me. Ten years with the man

I loved. Ten years of keeping my child from his father. I don't want you to make the same mistake."

Deanna shifted uncomfortably in her seat. She didn't want to discuss this. "Okay, I hear you. It's not like I'm kicking him to the curb or anything. But seriously, don't you think it's highly unlikely that I'm going to find lasting love at the same time you did?"

"Maybe it's fate," Natalie said, her eyes twinkling.

Deanna had thought fate had played a role in her life once before. When she had first gone to Hollywood. Instead, her heart had been ripped apart.

But she was ready to be done with this conversation, so she said, "I'm just taking it day by day. Now listen," she went on, wanting to change the subject to a more important matter. "I have an idea. I've been searching for our mother with no luck at all. And obviously neither you nor Nigel has had any luck. I'm thinking it's highly likely that our mother's original name wasn't Hart. In which case, it'll be all but impossible to find her. Your tracking her last steps in Philadelphia was definitely fate," Deanna said, looking at Natalie, "but we need more than fate to help us now. I'm thinking we should take our search public. You know, create a website. Do a video appeal. Heck, I'm sure we can get the media interested in this story. Because every lead so far has not worked out. I think this is our only shot."

Natalie nodded, a bright smile forming on her face. "That's an excellent idea, sis. Why didn't we think of that before?"

"It crossed my mind," Callie said. "But we run a risk with going public. Namely a gazillion crazy people coming forward claiming they have information."

"I know," Natalie said, "but what choice do we have?"

"Which is why I agree with the idea," Callie said. "We were hoping that Nigel and others would be able to track Mom down, but Deanna's right—that hasn't happened, and maybe our only option is the media."

"I'm convinced it's the only way," Deanna said. "Because of Natalie's search, we know that at least as of the time of Auntie Jean's death, our mother was in Philadelphia. Miss Dottie was certain of that. And she was equally certain that our mother was heading back to Georgia to deal with some unresolved issue. God only knows what that could be. I think it stands to reason that if she changed her name once, she may have changed it a few times. Clearly, Mom and Auntie Jean were running from something. An abusive father or mother. Maybe they were both in foster care. We don't know what their situation was. All we know is that they lived in Georgia. And that's not much to go on."

Natalie was nodding. "It's an excellent plan."

"I can call the guy who runs my website and have him set something up," Deanna offered. "Maybe we can name the website *searchforourmother.com* or something like that. I don't know. We'll do a video appeal, put it online. On the website, on YouTube and anywhere else we can think of. But I think the media will be our ticket to getting this story to spread nationwide."

"Yes," Callie agreed. "Fantastic idea."

"I just know this will work," Natalie said, squeezing Deanna's hand.

"I know it, too." It had to work.

The next day, Deanna went to speak to Kwame's class about her career. It was a Friday afternoon, and the moment Deanna entered the class, Kwame grinned from ear to ear. Then he ran to her and threw a hand around her waist. He was in his glory having Deanna in the class.

Anticipating her arrival, the kids were sitting on the floor in a semicircle, as opposed to at their desks.

"Class, I'm very excited that we have Ms. Hart with us today," the teacher, Mrs. Mortensen, said. "As you know, Ms. Hart is Kwame's aunt. She agreed to come and talk to you about her career."

One child's hand flew up immediately.

"Annabel, we're going to let Ms. Hart speak first before we ask questions. Okay?"

Annabel's hand went down.

"Ms. Hart, whenever you're ready. Perhaps you can tell the class about why you decided to pursue a career in music, what's it like, et cetera."

Deanna nodded. Then she grinned at the class of students, who were all wide-eyed, waiting for her to speak. It was nice that they were so interested in what she had to say.

"Well," she began, "as far back as I can remember, I always wanted to be a singer. I knew that it would mean hard work, and I wasn't even sure how I was going to make it happen. Of course, you all know about Hollywood?"

The kids nodded. Deanna continued. "Well, I realized that I would have to go to Hollywood if I was going to have a chance to make it as a singer."

Deanna suddenly wondered if she were speaking to the kids as though they were kindergartners. They seemed eager to hear what she had to say, but she decided to try a different tactic.

"What are some of your dreams?" she asked.

Annabel, the girl who had thrown her hand up immediately, was the first to do so now.

"I want to be a singer, too," she said.

"Really?" Deanna asked. When Annabel nodded, Deanna smiled at her, then looked around and chose a boy this time. "You?" she asked, pointing at him.

"I want to be an astronaut. I think it will be cool to go to the moon or Mars."

"Excellent," Deanna said.

"I want to be an actor."

"I want to be a veterinarian."

There were other answers—doctor, lawyer, artist. Deanna said, "Great. You all have goals. And that's the most important thing. That you know what you want to do. When I was young, I knew I wanted to be a singer. But like I said, I didn't know how I would make that happen. Then one day, I got the idea that I should head to Hollywood. In Hollywood, I could meet producers and other singers and managers. So that's what I did. I actually entered a talent competition I'd heard about—where I was able to sing. And while I didn't win the competition, I got the attention of a producer who agreed to work with me."

"Kind of like American Idol?" asked Kwame.

Deanna nodded. "Yes. I suppose so. Which goes to show that even if you don't do well on a show like that, you shouldn't be angry if you don't win. Because you can still take the opportunity to become successful."

There were nods of agreement, and then hands shot up. Even though Deanna hadn't quite finished her particular spiel, the kids were eager to ask their own questions.

She picked Annabel first, since the young girl had been so eager to have her question heard earlier. "Yes, Annabel?"

"What does it feel like, being famous?"

"That's the thing," Deanna began, "I don't feel any different. I still feel like the same person. I just sing for a living. I don't think that because I am a singer it makes me more special than anyone else." She paused, hoping she was getting that point across to the kids. All too often people sought out fame as a way to prove their self-worth. "What I will tell you is I feel awesome that I get to do what I love for a living— and that's something else to think about when you're thinking about your careers," Deanna said, because she knew that the teacher had wanted there to be a tie-in to career choices with this talk. "You have to choose something you really like to do. Something that you feel really excited about. Because if you don't like singing, yet you think that you should become one just because it's a cool career, then it won't be any fun for you. And you're probably not going to have success. What if you decide that you should become a doctor because doctors make a lot of money, yet you hate the sight of blood? If you decide to become a doctor and you hate blood, how is that going to work? You can't just choose a career because you think that you're going to make a lot of money doing it."

"How much money do you make?" came the question from one boy.

The teacher looked at him with a chastising expression. "Nathan," she began, "we talked about that before Ms. Hart got here, right? Certain questions are considered polite, and others aren't, remember?"

Nathan nodded, but he was frowning as he lowered his hand.

"What I can tell you, Nathan," Deanna began, "is that you can make a good living at a career like being a singer. And no, not everybody's going to make millions and millions of dollars like you see some of the rappers and other artists making. Only some people become superstars. I wasn't a superstar, but I was happy. I did well."

A girl chimed, "My mother thinks you're a superstar. She loves your music. She plays it all the time. She even went to one of your concerts."

"Really?" Deanna asked, a smile touching her lips. "Well, you tell your mother that I'm thankful for that."

The questions continued, the normal sort of thing she was used to—where did she get her ideas, what famous people had she worked with? She answered them all, and the kids were excited to know that she had met some of the music industry's biggest stars.

"Are you going back to Hollywood?" asked one girl, who almost seemed unhappy as she asked the question. As if the idea that Deanna might leave town was disappointing to her.

"I suppose I will, one day." And for some reason, she thought about Eric as she said the words. Swallowing, she went on. "But for now, I'm happy to be here. And as I'm sure you already know, I'm working with the eighth-grade students on their musical. So I've been at the school quite a lot."

"What about when you finish the play?" Nathan asked. "Will you still work at the school?"

"Maybe she can be a music teacher," one girl suggested.

A buzz of excitement spread through the room as the kids suggested more ideas that would keep Deanna around, which did her heart good. Mrs. Mortensen had to get everyone back on track, after which Deanna answered more questions. And then, after many requests, she agreed to perform one of her songs.

It was a slow number called "Falling in Love," about a woman who found love where she least expected it. As she sang, Deanna turned toward the classroom door.

And her heart thundered in her chest when she saw Eric standing there, watching.

When she was finished singing, the kids erupted in applause. Looking in the direction of the door again, Deanna noticed that Eric was gone.

Mrs. Mortensen approached her and pumped her hand several times. "It was such a pleasure," she said. "I'm so glad you came to talk to the students." And then the woman smiled somewhat bashfully. "I'm a fan, too," she added.

"I'm happy to be here."

"Would you mind signing autographs for the students?"

Mrs. Mortensen asked. "I told them I'd ask you at the end, if there was time. And if you agreed."

"Absolutely," Deanna said.

Mrs. Mortensen smiled sheepishly. "Maybe you can also sign one for me?"

"Of course."

Once Deanna left Kwame's classroom, she headed to the office. She had her overnight bag packed for their getaway, in case Eric wanted to leave directly from the school.

"Hello, Michelle," Deanna said brightly as she entered the office. She had decided not to take offence at the woman's supposed change in attitude since they'd met. If she had a crush on Eric and he didn't return her affections…well, that had to be hard to deal with.

And maybe because Deanna had been warm with her greeting, Michelle actually gave her a genuine smile. "Hiya. How did it go in Kwame's class?"

"It was excellent," Deanna replied. "Really fun."

"And the rehearsals are coming along well, I hear."

"Yeah." Deanna nodded.

"Not missing Hollywood?"

"Actually, I'm enjoying working with the students more than I expected." She shrugged. "Maybe I missed my calling."

"Oh, I'm sure you'll be back in Hollywood soon enough." Her voice held a note of hopefulness. "The paycheck is better."

"As hard as this may be to believe, I never got into music for the money. Hollywood is so vibrant and full of life…but it also has its dark side." She paused. "And as for working with the kids, it's exactly what I need right now." She didn't add that it was providing her an escape from the dark side she had personally experienced in Hollywood.

Michelle nodded, but she seemed distracted as her gaze

wandered off. And then the brightest of smiles formed on her face. Deanna turned, following the woman's line of sight.

And she saw Eric outside of the office's glass walls.

If Deanna had had any doubt before, she no longer did. Michelle most definitely had a thing for Eric.

Should she really be surprised? Eric was gorgeous, single and a great catch. It certainly made sense that someone who got to see him day in and day out would have a little crush on him.

But Eric's smile was definitely for Deanna only. "Hey, Deanna." And in a lower voice he said, "You ready for this weekend?"

"This weekend?" Michelle asked, sounding both intrigued and confused.

Deanna looked in her direction, wishing that Eric hadn't said anything in front of Michelle.

Eric faced Michelle, whose smile was faltering. "Yeah," he said, clearing his throat. "Deanna and I have plans."

"Oh." Michelle definitely didn't look happy, but the phone rang, and she quickly answered it.

With a jerk of his head, Eric gestured toward his office. Deanna followed him in there, and he immediately put his hands on her shoulders. "You ready?" he asked, his voice still low.

"I'm packed and ready to go."

"Good. Meet me at my house at six, okay?"

"All right. I can do that." And then she said quietly, "What's up with Michelle?"

Eric shook his head. "Don't worry about her."

Deanna began to nod. "Okay. I'll see you later."

As she left Eric's office, she couldn't help noting that Michelle's expression was sour now.

"I'll bet he's taking you to the cabin," Michelle said.

Deanna paused mid-step. "Excuse me?"

"His cabin on Lake Erie," she said, her voice now holding a hint of smugness. "It's really nice, I'm sure you'll like it there."

Deanna was so startled, she didn't know what to say. So she said, "See you next week."

And then she quickly headed out the door.

Chapter 13

Deanna met Eric at his house at six o'clock, and together they got into his Ford Explorer. Michelle's comment had disturbed her, and she tried to tell herself that the woman was just trying to get under her skin. Clearly, Michelle didn't like the fact that Deanna and Eric had gotten close. She told herself not to bring up the issue with Eric.

"So, will you tell me exactly where we're going?" Deanna asked.

"Just about thirty minutes away," Eric answered. "In West-lake."

"Pricey neighborhood," Deanna said, emitting a low whistle. "Michael Jones has a home there. A large, sprawling estate on the water. It's gorgeous."

"I'm taking you to my parents' cottage, and it's nothing like Michael's place. But it's on the lake, which is very nice. It's small, just a couple of bedrooms, but it's on an acre of land. My parents invested in the real estate market for a number of years and did very well. Then they bought this house on the water, which they renovated and treat as a home away from home. Only thirty minutes outside of Cleveland, but it's like a whole new world. Very serene."

"Sounds lovely," Deanna said.

"It is," Eric concurred. "They plan to sell it, but want to wait until the economy is better."

Deanna nodded. "Ah."

Eric reached for her hand and linked fingers with hers. Deanna stared down at their joined hands, and she suddenly felt a pang of longing. That longing to have a relationship that was real, that would last forever.

Had she found that with Eric?

"You're going to love it."

At Eric's comment, Deanna's stomach constricted. The words made her think of what Michelle had said, and she could no longer hold her tongue.

Turning to Eric, she said, "Eric, Michelle said something odd to me." She drew in a deep breath. "She told me to enjoy my time at the cabin with you. That it was beautiful. Obviously, she's been there with you..." Her voice trailed off, but her question was clear.

"Michelle and the rest of the staff came to the house last June, at the end of school. I had a party for everyone there."

Relief washed over Deanna. "Oh. *Oh*."

"You sound relieved. What were you thinking?"

"I...I didn't know what to think." She paused, then decided to go for honesty. "Okay, I'm still thinking that your secretary has a crush on you."

"I think maybe she does, too," Eric conceded. "It's harmless."

"I get the sense," Deanna went on, "that she's not happy about us. The whole thing about letting me know she'd been to the cabin...I'm sure she was trying to make me jealous."

"And did it work?" Eric asked.

"Wh-what?"

"Did it work? Did she make you jealous?"

Deanna wasn't quite sure what to say. "Of course not," she hedged.

"No, of course not," Eric said, and Deanna picked up on a hint of dissatisfaction in his tone. "Not when we're just friends with benefits, right?"

Eric was only repeating Deanna's mantra, but for some reason the words stung.

"So it wouldn't bother you to know that I kissed her, then?"

Now Deanna jerked her gaze to Eric's. "You...when?"

"Last year," Eric admitted. "We went out. I guess I wanted to see if there was anything between us. But I felt nothing."

"And that's all? Only that one kiss?"

"Yes," Eric told her.

Deanna settled her head back against the headrest, thinking that Eric must think she was a mess. If she really only believed them to be friends with benefits, she shouldn't be in the least concerned about anything that had happened with him and Michelle.

Thankfully, Eric changed the subject. "The musical is coming along quite well," Eric said. "I'm really impressed."

"Yes," Deanna agreed, smiling. "I'm very pleased."

"Your hard work has made all the difference," Eric went on. "The kids sound like pros."

"The kids are super-talented. I'm only helping to bring out what they're capable of." She paused. "I never imagined I'd ever be working with kids in this capacity, but I'm having the best time. Even talking to Kwame's class today...it was really special."

"You want kids?" Eric asked.

Deanna hesitated. It was a question she had asked herself before, and she had never been certain. "Truthfully, there was a time I didn't think I'd ever want children," she told him. "Never knowing my father, my mother leaving me and my sisters…I never wanted to have children and know that I might do something that disappointed them or broke their hearts. But now…spending time with Kwame, seeing how resilient he's been after not knowing his father…well, I'm not so sure anymore."

"Why would you disappoint your children?" Eric asked her. "Just because your mother hurt you doesn't mean you'll hurt your kids."

"I know, it doesn't make sense. It's just…knowing how much a child depends on you. But who knows?" She shrugged.

Eric squeezed her hand, a supportive gesture.

"What about you?" she asked him. "Do you want kids?" But before he could answer, she did. "Yes, I'm sure you—"

The ringing of Deanna's phone interrupted her, and she stopped. Then she reached into her purse. She dug out her phone, saying, "That's probably Callie. She said she'd call someone at a local news station about doing a story regarding our mother."

But when Deanna looked at the caller ID, her heart froze. It was Brian's number flashing on the screen. She hadn't bothered to block his calls, thinking he would only phone her from another number until she picked up.

"Deanna?" Eric asked when the phone stopped ringing. When she didn't speak, his tone became more urgent. "Deanna, you okay?"

Deanna shook her head, her stomach constricting. She didn't understand what was going on. Why Brian was suddenly contacting her again.

The phone began to ring again, and Deanna's chest tightened along with her stomach.

"It's him, isn't it?" Eric asked. And before Deanna could utter a word, Eric took the phone from her. "Brian," Eric said with distaste. Then he pressed the talk button. "I don't know what your problem is, but stop calling this phone. You keep harassing Deanna, and I'm going to have to do something about it. Consider this fair warning."

Then Eric ended the call.

Deanna looked over at him in a state of shock. A part of her had been seized with fear when Eric answered the phone, but slowly, relief was coming over her. Maybe that was exactly what Brian needed—to hear the voice of another man. Maybe he would finally get the picture.

Deanna released a breath she didn't know she'd been holding. "What did he say?"

"Nothing. No doubt he was shocked to hear me on the line." Eric smoothed his thumb over the top of her hand. "But I'm betting that now he'll leave you alone."

"God, I hope so."

There had been no further talk about Brian as they drove, but Eric had felt the man's presence in the car nonetheless. Deanna had at first seemed relieved that he'd spoken to him, but then she had become quiet. Every time Eric looked at her, he could see worry lines etched on her forehead.

So when they got to the cottage, he exited the vehicle and immediately went to her. He put his arm around her waist as he walked with her to the front door. And touching her like that, Eric could feel her body trembling.

"Damn it, Deanna," Eric said once he opened the door and led her inside. "You've got to tell me what's going on here. You're shaking like you're afraid. Did more happen with Brian than you've told me?"

She wandered to the nearby sofa, where she sat and hugged her knees to her chest. "I've told you everything. Except... except that he called me a couple of times a few weeks ago. I just don't understand why he's bothering me all of a sudden."

Eric fumed. It was bad enough that Brian had had the nerve to put his hands on this beautiful woman. But to be harassing her months after the fact—if he dared to come near her now and try to harm her, it would be the last thing he ever did.

"Well, now I've spoken to him. Maybe he'll be more likely to leave you alone now, knowing that he'll have to go through me before he can get to you."

"I hope so," Deanna said. "But...but what if he gets angrier?"

"I meant what I said to him," Eric said with conviction. "If he comes near you, he's going to have to deal with me." He paused. "All the same, I agree that you have every reason not to trust him. In fact, I would feel better if you stayed at my place. That way I can watch over you, protect you."

Eric saw Deanna's eyes widen with curiosity. "You want me to move into your place?"

It hadn't been what he'd expected to say, but Eric found himself nodding. He wanted her in his life in every way. He wanted her in his bed each night, to see her every morning. He wanted to take care of her and protect her. Despite the fact that she had made sure to remind him that they were only friends with benefits, his feelings weren't changing. In fact, they were deepening.

"All I know is that I want you near me," he told her. "And this Brian idiot is out there, a threat to you—that's all the more reason for you to stay with me. That way I can protect you."

"My knight in shining armor?" Deanna offered him a small smile.

And just that little smile brightened his mood. Sinking onto the sofa beside her, Eric placed a gentle hand on her leg. With the other hand, he turned her chin toward him and kissed her.

Deanna ended the kiss abruptly, and Eric gave her a questioning look. That's when he saw the worried look on her face.

"Something's not right," Eric said. "You keep telling me that there's nothing more to what happened with this Brian guy, but I'm not sure that's true."

"It's just…"

Eric slipped his arm around her back and pulled her close. "Just what?"

"It's… I think I told you, after Brian assaulted me, I started having nightmares? Well, they're getting more intense. I suppose because he called me out of the blue. I don't know."

Eric sensed there was more. "What is it you're not telling me?"

"Well, it's weird. But last night, for the first time since I started having the dreams, it almost seemed to me that I wasn't dreaming about Brian assaulting me. In fact, I got a glimpse of somebody else. Another man's face."

Eric stared at her with wonder. "You think that means something?"

"I don't know. Maybe." She shrugged. "All I know is that something about this dream is extremely unsettling to me. I feel…like there's a sense of unfinished business." She made a face, as though her own words were confusing to her. "I know that must sound crazy."

"You're suffering from a little post-traumatic stress," Eric told her. "And that only makes sense. But please know, nobody is going to hurt you now. Not while I'm here to do something about it."

"You're very sweet," Deanna told him. But her eyes were sad, and Eric got the distinct feeling that there was even more she wasn't saying. Even the way she was leaning away from him told him that. And although they were here together for a romantic weekend, he could tell that Brian's call had put a wedge between them.

"Why do I think there's still more you're not telling me?" he said gently. "There was a time when you trusted me with everything, remember? Now, it's like no matter how much I'm trying to get close to you on a deeper level, you have a wall up."

"I guess…I guess Brian's calls have made me think of something else, too."

"What?" Eric asked.

Deanna sighed. "Of the people I trusted in Hollywood… people I trusted who hurt me."

"So there is something else," Eric stated.

Deanna nodded. "But maybe you can pour us some wine first? I'm going to need it for this one."

A short while later, Deanna was holding her glass of red wine, and Eric was sitting beside her again, but this time with a little space between them.

"You were saying?" Eric prompted.

"When I first went to L.A., I was full of hope. In a way, I was running—running from what Marvin had done to me, running from my past where my own mother had abandoned me—and I met someone. Someone who made me hope."

Deanna paused. Eric simply stared at her. Then he said, "Go on."

"His name was Mason Lee. And he was older than Marvin. Older than any guy I'd dated before. Nearly twenty-two years older than me, he was in his early forties. But I didn't care. In fact, I thought that a man of his age wouldn't be into games. Wouldn't break my heart."

"But he did break your heart."

Deanna sipped her wine. She hadn't thought about Mason in a long time. And the fact that she was sharing this story made her wonder if his betrayal still hurt her at this point in her life.

But maybe she had never really dealt with his betrayal, just tried to bury the pain.

She drew in a deep breath and then continued. "I wanted to become a singer. He said he could make it happen. It was a chance meeting after I signed up for a competition. Something through an agency that put a bunch of hopefuls in front of producers and agents. Mason took a liking to me. He told me that he could make me a star.

"He was sophisticated, he knew the business. And he had so much faith in me. He invested in me. Got me a vocal coach, put time and energy and money into me to get me to do my first demo. Probably four months passed, and everything was happening for me so easily. Because of Mason. In a way, I suppose I looked at him as a father figure. Stable, secure, protective. He gave me my dream. And when he told me that he was in love with me…"

"Wow," Eric muttered.

"Please," Deanna said. "Don't judge me before you've heard the story."

"I'm not judging you. I'm judging him."

"Let me finish," Deanna said. The truth was, she felt stupid after what had happened with Mason. He had seemed so completely wonderful…but he turned out to be nothing more than a liar. At least when it came to being able to trust him with her heart.

"I felt I owed him. But more than that, I cared for him. It wasn't hard for me to think that he and I could be great together. He had worked with me to get my first album together. And suddenly, out of nowhere, I was somebody in the industry. I saw no reason why we shouldn't work. In fact, I think I'd developed a crush on him long before he told me how he felt."

Eric gritted his teeth, but he said nothing.

"So I moved into this place with him. A huge, beautiful home. I felt like Cinderella. I'd met my Prince Charming. Everything in my life was going well. I was an adult—who cared that he was two decades older than I was? That didn't matter. Age was only number, after all."

Again, Deanna paused. Eric said quietly, "Go on."

"For a year, we were happy. I thought nothing could be better than that. I had mixed business with pleasure—something I was too young to even be wary of doing—but it was all working out. Mason was my producer, my manager and my love. He even proposed to me. You don't understand. I was young in Hollywood with a dream—so many others go there and leave heartbroken. I had one chance meeting with the man who changed it all for me. Changed it for the better. I was on cloud nine. And like I said, I felt that I owed him. But more than that, I put my wall down with him because he seemed to respect me. He cared about me so much that he put everything into investing in me. And because of him, I caught that star that ninety-nine percent of wannabes only hope to catch."

"How did he hurt you? That's all I care about."

Deanna was surprised to find that a tear was trickling down her cheek. It was just that she didn't like to think about Mason. She didn't like to think about the young girl she had been, so full of hope. So full of trust in the man who seemed to have it all together. "It was about eight months into our living together that I learned he was sleeping with someone else. And not just someone else. There were other girls. Other girls like me. Young, with stars in their eyes, hoping for that break in Hollywood." Deanna brushed her tear away angrily, because certainly Mason didn't deserve them. He was a jerk of the highest order. "He was sleeping with all of them."

"Wow."

"I'm sure you think I'm stupid," Deanna said. "That I should have known better."

"What I think, Deanna, is that that guy was a world-class

prick. A predator. Sure, you may have been old enough, but he preyed on you. Just as he preyed on those other young girls."

"After that, I knew that I should have been smart enough not to mix business with pleasure. I could have saved myself the heartache."

"I wish I could say I'm surprised by Mason's behavior," Eric said, "but I'm not. Some men—men like my brother— seem to live to take advantage of women. Maybe that's why I've been so different in my own life. I never wanted to see a woman look at me with pain in her eyes the way I saw you look at me after Marvin hurt you. The way I saw Beverly look at me after Marvin hurt her."

Now, Eric eased closer to Deanna. "That wasn't about mixing business with pleasure. It was about choosing the wrong guy. But Deanna, you have to forgive yourself. You were young, naive. Mason saw that and took advantage of it."

Deanna knew that Eric was right. She told herself that after a couple of years had passed and she'd been able to look back on her relationship with Mason with some perspective. She had told herself that, and yet she still felt guilty.

"It's just...I let my walls down completely with him. And he destroyed me." She paused. "I was incredibly naive. So since then I've thought that maybe my need to hope was going to lead to heartache over and over again. I wanted to believe that my mother was coming back when she said she was. She never did. My mother hurt me. And then my sister—she knew how much Marvin meant to me, and yet she still hurt me. And then Mason. Not to mention that my father didn't want to stick around in my life."

"You've been hurt. Time and time again."

Deanna nodded. "Yes."

"Do you think I'm going to hurt you, too?"

"Maybe," Deanna said softly, surprised at the answer that had slipped from her lips.

Eric shook his head, a look of hurt and dismay coming over his face. "After everything, I can't believe you would say that."

"It's not that I believe that. God, Eric—don't you know I realize that you're the one man I've been able to rely on? At least when we were just friends, I was certain of things between us. Now…well, now we've entered scary territory. And I'm desperately afraid that things will change between us."

"Nothing has changed. Nothing will change. I'm not going to hurt you."

"I don't look at you and think, *I can't trust him.* It's myself I can't trust. My track record has shown that when it comes to men, I don't have the judgment."

"Damn."

"I don't mean it that way. Please, I'm not talking about you. I'm not trying to offend you, lump you in with all other men. This isn't about you. It's about me. That's what I'm trying to say. Maybe I could screw up a relationship with even the nicest guy in the world." And when she felt her eyes mist, she brushed at them and uttered, "Oh, God."

"Hey," Eric said, his voice soft, his touch on her cheek equally soft. "You did not deserve what happened to you. What your mother did, what your sister did, what Mason did, what Brian did—heck, my brother, too. You didn't deserve it." He paused. "In fact, you're stronger than you realize. Despite being hurt, you still put your heart out there, risking being hurt again. And that's the way it ought to be. Because you can't close your heart off. That's no kind of life."

Deanna heard the words. And she tried to breathe them in, hold them in her heart and allow them to truly sink in and penetrate.

Because she knew that Eric was right.

And what Eric was saying was allowing her a chance to heal.

Deanna awoke with a start. For a moment she didn't know where she was.

But when she realized that there was a warm leg pressed against hers, she instantly remembered.

She was with Eric. In his parents' cottage.

Based on the fact that they were both in the bed, and the room was dark, it was clearly the middle of the night. Deanna glanced at the digital clock on the nightstand, which confirmed her thought. It was 3:14 in the morning.

Snippets of last night came back to her. Eric talking to her about Brian. Asking her to move in with him so he could protect her. Deanna telling him about the dream and wondering if it meant something more. Then telling him the story about Mason, which perhaps hurt the most.

Eric had been the perfect gentleman, holding her and comforting her, when she was certain that he had had a lot more than cuddling in mind.

Deanna rolled over now, placed her head on his chest. He stirred. Then he snaked his hand around her waist, but she wasn't sure if that were simply a gesture in sleep or if he were awake.

"Hey," Deanna whispered in the darkened room.

"Hmm?" came Eric's groggy reply.

Deanna eased herself upward so that her head was now next to his. "Are you sleeping?"

A brief pause. Then, "Not anymore."

"Good," she told him, pressing her lips against his.

And then she climbed on top of him.

"Ohh," said Eric, putting his hands on her hips.

"Ohh," Deanna echoed and giggled. And then she began to kiss him deeply, and her giggles soon turned into sighs.

Chapter 14

Eric and Deanna spent Saturday doing what any hot-blooded man and woman would do alone in a cabin.

Making love.

They walked the grounds, of course, and Deanna discovered that Eric's description of the place was on point. It was serene.

If there wasn't a chill coming off of the water, Deanna would have enjoyed making love near the shore. The cottage certainly had the privacy. Instead, she and Eric walked along the water's edge and necked like a couple of teenagers.

Then they went back into the cabin and made love again.

There was a Jacuzzi on the large back patio, and it was beautiful looking out at the changing colors of the leaves while being naked in a Jacuzzi tub with your lover.

It had been a day of romance, and Eric had thought of everything. Strawberries and whipped cream. Champagne.

"You take romance to a whole new level," Deanna told him

as he dipped a strawberry in the whipped cream and then fed it to her as they later lay on a soft rug in front of the fireplace.

"You think so?"

"Uh-huh."

Then Eric dipped another strawberry in whipped cream, but instead of putting it in Deanna's mouth, he twirled it around her nipple…and proceeded to lick it off.

Sexually, it had been the best day of her life. Physically, she had been pleased beyond measure—over and over again. Emotionally…well, she had finally started to let her guard down.

Eric was an amazing man, and he was into her. And as much as she had insisted that they were friends with bene-fits, she no longer felt anxiety at the thought that Eric was a lot more than that to her.

On Sunday morning, Deanna got up earlier than Eric and planned to spend the day pampering him. She got out the eggs and ham slices and cheese, planning to make him the best omelet he'd ever tasted.

"Wow."

At the sound of Eric's voice, Deanna turned around. "Morning."

A smile on his face, he began to approach her. "Now this is a sight I could get used to. Seeing you standing naked in the kitchen…"

"I'm making you breakfast."

"You're going to stand over a stove wearing nothing at all?"

"I was checking to see what items you had. Now that I know, I'm planning to put a robe on."

"No." Eric's voice was husky as he slipped his arms around her waist. "That won't do."

With difficulty, Deanna groaned and then eased out of Eric's arms. "I want this to be perfect for you."

"Oh, it's perfect all right."

She started for the bedroom. "How many times did we make love yesterday? You can't actually be excited seeing me naked again!"

"Naked, clothed—I'm always excited around you."

The words sent an electric charge through her. And the look in Eric's eyes as he advanced, the look of lustful determination…well, it was her undoing.

"I suppose breakfast could wait," she said, lowering herself onto the bed.

"You're the only thing I'm hungry for," Eric told her, and then he brought his mouth down on hers and kissed her hard.

An hour later, Eric had just headed into the shower when Deanna's cell phone rang. And when she saw Brian's name on the screen, unease gripped her.

But so did anger. Why was he harassing her? Deanna had to put a stop to this, and now.

So she answered the phone. "Brian, you have to stop calling me."

"Who was that guy who answered the phone?" he asked.

"This is the last conversation we're ever going to have—do you understand me?"

"I need you here," Brian said. "Back in Hollywood. The deal is back on. I've renegotiated a better deal for you, babe—and get this, it's for two more CDs. It's a great deal."

Was Brian insane? "Did you hear me? We're over, done—and I sure as hell won't be doing any business with you."

"You're blowing off this deal?" Brian asked. "After I went out of my way to get this worked out for you?"

"After you screwed it up in the first place!" Deanna countered. She glanced over her shoulder, hoping that Eric was not exiting the bathroom. But she could still hear the water running in the shower, which was good.

"You ungrateful— You used me to further your career and then dumped me."

"You're insane, Brian," Deanna said. "You know that's not how it happened."

"Do you want this career or don't you?" Brian countered.

"I am not going back to L.A. I'm not working with you again."

"Because of that guy who answered the phone?" Brian asked disbelievingly. Then he laughed, a condescending sound. "Does he know your track record? That you stay with a guy, use him until you get bored, then you move on?" When Deanna said nothing, Brian went on. "What—you didn't know that guys talk? Well, they do. And you have quite the reputation. I'm not the only guy whose heart you broke. The only one you used. Mason Lee gave you your shot in this business, and you dumped him the moment you became successful."

Hearing the name of the man Deanna had foolishly trusted when she first got to Los Angeles made her stomach lurch—especially when Brian was acting as though she had somehow wronged the egomaniac music producer.

"Are you trying to get revenge on every man because your daddy left you? Don't forget—your mother left you, too. Obviously with good reason," Brian finished, dealing the final blow.

"D-don't say that to me," Deanna said.

"I tried to love you," Brian went on. "But some people just aren't worthy of love."

And then silence.

Brian had hung up on her. After everything he'd said, he had been the one to have the satisfaction of hanging up on her.

Tears filled Deanna's eyes, and she gripped the counter. Everything she had told Brian, her deepest fears and darkest pain that she had confessed during their pillow talk after sex, he had just thrown back in her face.

She knew he was trying to hurt her.

And yet, she was defenseless against his assault. Because he had just reminded her of her biggest fear—that no one would love her forever.

Her father had left her, her mother, too.

How long before Eric did the same?

Deanna glanced toward the bathroom. She could still hear the shower running. Suddenly, she knew she had to leave. She quickly gathered her belongings and headed out of the cabin. Eric had driven them here, and she knew it was a long walk to the road, but she had to get out of there.

Eric wouldn't understand, she knew that. But she suddenly felt as if she was drowning. She had to get out of this cabin and all the dreams and hopes it represented.

She couldn't believe in those hopes and dreams.

Deanna hurried outside. She jogged along the road that led to the main road. Eric had stopped at a gas station maybe a mile away where he'd picked up a couple of things before they got to the cabin. If she could make it there, she would have a place where a taxi could pick her up that wasn't the side of an unfamiliar road.

Tears fell from Deanna's eyes, but she brushed them away. Why was she crying? She knew good and well that she shouldn't have put her wall down with Eric.

And no, he wasn't hurting her. She was distinctly aware that she was the one who would be disappointing him. But it was best that they put an immediate halt to things. Go back to being friends with benefits without the emotional complications. Better yet, go back to being just friends.

It was the only thing Deanna knew of that would ensure the protection of her heart.

Eric exited the bathroom feeling refreshed and energized. He was ready to eat the breakfast Deanna had prepared, which would provide sustenance for the next round. He had made love to her for hours already, but it was not enough. He needed to feel her beneath him, against him, on top of him again.

He had never felt this sexually satisfied, not even when he'd been married. Which only served to prove the point that he had been with the wrong woman.

Deanna, however, he felt was right. She always had been.

Eric dried himself off with a towel, and contemplated walking out to Deanna without a stitch of clothing on. He wanted to see the reaction in her eyes, the moment her surprised look turned to a lustful one. And then he would take her back to bed, take her clothes off and slowly please her until they were both physically spent.

But instead, he dried himself off and decided to do the more modest thing. He wrapped the towel around his waist and exited the bathroom, saying, "Hey, babe."

He didn't see her in the kitchen, so he turned and looked in the living room area. She wasn't there, either.

And then he understood. A grin forming on his face, he realized that Deanna must have been thinking what he had a moment ago…that she wanted to get naked again. So he walked into the bedroom, certain that he would see her there, looking comfortable on the bed. He had contemplated surprising her, but it seemed she was the one who had surprised him again.

He went to the bedroom and walked through the open door, ready to see her naked and waiting for him. But instead, he saw an empty room. He wasn't discouraged. She couldn't have gone too far, he thought. But when he looked around the bedroom, she wasn't there.

That was when he got the first niggling sense of concern.

As he continued to search, his panic began to set in. And soon, a search of every corner of the house proved that she was not anywhere.

"What the heck?" he uttered aloud.

Maybe she was on the front porch. He quickly hurried to the front door, opened it, but she was nowhere to be found. He then went to the back door where the Jacuzzi was. Yes, he told himself, feeling foolish. Of course she was in the Jacuzzi. What had taken him so long to figure it out?

Opening the back door, Eric prepared to tell Deanna how much of a fright she'd given him.

But the words died in his throat when he saw that she wasn't out there, either.

What was going on? He began to call out her name. "Deanna! Deanna!" He listened for sound, for a response from her. There was none. He went back into the house and again called out to her. He knew it wasn't likely that they had just missed paths while he opened one door and she opened another. But it wasn't impossible. So he called out to her again, hoping that she would respond.

All he got was silence.

Eric rushed back into his bedroom now, where he dropped the towel. He quickly found some clothes and hurriedly put them on while heading toward the front door. Then he charged outside, frowning when he got to the driveway at the side of the house.

He had almost expected his vehicle to be gone, but it was still there. *Where on earth would she have gone?* They were at a remote cabin. It wasn't impossible that she could walk to the main road, but how long would that take?

And why would she? Why would she be so desperate to get away from him, at a moment when he'd believed everything was going as well as it could be?

Eric went back into the house. He was going to get his car keys, jump into his vehicle and find her. But something made him stop before heading outside again. Because he realized that if she had left him like this—and on foot—it meant one thing.

She had wanted to get away.

And if she was so desperate to leave him, then what kind of fool would he be to chase her down? He had done everything to make her feel secure, hadn't he? To show her that he was the same man from years ago whom she could trust. The only difference now was that he had made it clear that he felt something more for her.

Though Eric wanted to go after her, track her down and shake some sense into her, he didn't. Instead, he sank onto the sofa with a heavy heart.

One minute Deanna had been moaning in his arms as he gave her pleasure—pleasure she claimed she'd never felt in her life before—and now she was gone. He didn't understand it.

But if she was going to this extreme to run from him, then he would have to let her walk. He would have to let her go.

Perhaps she had simply gone out to wander to the grounds alone. Maybe she wanted to pick some fall flowers or just enjoy the beauty of the nature surrounding them on her own.

In which case she would be coming back.

Eric resolved to wait for her inside the cabin. But when the minutes ticked by turning into one hour, and then one hour rolled into two, he knew.

She had left him.

Chapter 15

Deanna was in a slump. Yes, she had been the one to walk away from Eric at the cabin—*run* was more like it—but she was disappointed that he hadn't tried to call her.

Her rational brain knew that she was the one who ought to call him. In fact, she should have shown up on his doorstep Sunday evening and pleaded with him for a chance to explain. But she hadn't.

And now it was Monday afternoon, and everything was set in motion to work on the video appeal Deanna and her sisters were going to put online.

Deanna, Callie and Natalie were assembled at their uncle's house, the three of them on the front porch as Nigel's videographer friend, Stan, positioned them.

"You want to be standing, sitting?" Stan asked.

"Whatever is fine," Deanna said.

"I think we should be standing." Natalie faced her sisters, giving them a questioning look. "Sitting is too casual, don't you think? And maybe we should be standing closer to the street so that you can get a better view of the house," she added.

Callie nodded. "That sounds good to me. Our mother will see the house, see that we're all here. That we're together."

Deanna only hoped that she would see it.

Once Stan had them positioned just right, he instructed them to begin talking. "Speak from the heart. Say whatever you want to say."

Callie, the oldest, led the charge. "Mom, this is Callie. I'm sure you remember me. It's been twenty-three years, but I know you could never forget us. We're back here, at Auntie Jean's house. I'm not sure why you ran, but we know you were in some sort of trouble. What we want you to know is that we don't care what the trouble was. We don't care about your past, about what might have happened. We love you. And we want you to come back."

Deanna was nodding her head in agreement. "Yes, Callie's right. You're our mother. Our blood. Nothing that has happened in the past would ever make us not want to reunite with you."

"We love you," Natalie chimed in. "Twenty-three years ago you left saying that you would be back soon. I want you to know that I never gave up believing that you would come back. We've been searching for you, not knowing if you were dead or alive. And when I found out that you were alive even a few months ago, you don't know how elated I was. I know you're out there, and that we'll find you. If you're seeing this, please, come back. Come back to us."

The three sisters continued to speak from their hearts, leaving the email address of the website that Deanna's webmaster had set up as a contact. They also told her she could contact the police and ask for Nigel Williams, because they didn't want to leave Uncle Dave's phone number. However, it had not changed since the day they had been dropped off twenty-three years ago, and Callie ended by saying to their mother that she could still call that number to reach them. Hopefully their mother would still remember it, and if not, she could always email or contact the police station.

"That was great," Stan said. "Really heartfelt, wonderful. I'll get that footage edited and up on the website by tomorrow morning."

"Excellent," Deanna said. Her stomach was fluttering. She was nervous. Every part of her told her that this was it. This was the piece of the puzzle needed to find their mother. She would see the appeal, and she would come for them.

"And then the media interview tomorrow evening," Callie said, emitting a ragged breath.

"Tomorrow at five," Deanna concurred. She and her sisters had wanted to have the website up and running, plus the video appeal up, before doing an interview for the news. That way they could mention the website on the news.

"This is it, guys," Natalie said. "She's going to see this, and she's going to come back to us."

Michael, who was there for support, slipped his arms around Natalie's waist. And then she began to cry softly and turned her face against his chest, taking comfort from his strength.

A lump formed in Deanna's throat when she regarded her sister and Michael. All she could think about was Eric and how she had left him at the cabin.

She wanted what her sisters had found…and in her heart, she knew she had it with Eric. But something was holding her back. Something beyond the fear that things would go wrong.

Still, she felt like a louse for the way she'd left him, and she wondered now if she ought to go see him, apologize— that is, if he'd even want to see her.

An apology could hardly suffice for what she had done.

* * *

Deanna felt even worse the next day, but she tried to concentrate on the task at hand—finding her mother.

The three major networks sent out reporters to cover the story, surely Deanna's star power helped, and this time as the sisters appealed to their mother to come home, there were tears.

Again, Nigel and Michael were there for her sisters, but Deanna was alone. And she felt it.

She felt it so much that when she caught the first glimpse of Eric approaching the house, she was certain she had imagined him. But he took more steps toward her, and her heart filled with hope when she realized that indeed it was Eric.

He had come.

Her spirits lifted immediately, and she smiled. Then she bounded toward him, her arms outstretched. He immediately wrapped her in a hug.

"Eric." She held him, drawing strength from his arms.

"Kwame told me you were doing this," he said. "I…I wanted to be here."

"I'm glad you came." She eased back and looked up at him. "I…I'm sorry. I…know that's not enough, but I am."

"How did the interview go?" Eric asked, not addressing her apology.

"It went well." She bobbed her head up and down. "We're really excited. We all feel that this is it. We're going to find our mother."

"Good." Eric ran a hand over her shoulder and down her arm. It was a supportive gesture, and yet she could still feel the barrier between them.

No surprise there. She was entirely to blame for it.

"Excuse me," Eric said, stepping away from her.

Deanna hugged her torso as she watched him approach her sisters and greet them. Then he shook hands with Michael and Nigel and said words to them that Deanna couldn't hear from her vantage point.

Finally, he came back over to her. "Um," she began, "maybe we can head back to your place?"

"No," Eric said, not even considering her suggestion for a second. "I don't think that's a good idea."

Deanna's heart fell. She felt incredibly foolish for her behavior on Sunday. She'd just panicked, and she wanted to make Eric understand. "I just…I owe you an explanation…I figured we could talk."

"Then we can talk in my car," Eric suggested.

"Okay." Deanna found herself nodding, but she was suddenly scared. He was far too serious, far too grim. Had she completely blown things with him?

She followed him to his car. When he opened the passenger door, she got in. Then Eric rounded the car and got in beside her.

"I can't say sorry enough," she said to him once he closed the door. "I…I got scared."

Eric said nothing.

"I think my talking to you about everything really shook me. Made me remember all the bad things in my life. It took me to a really dark place."

Eric still said nothing, just regarded her.

"Eric…say something," Deanna said, keeping her tone light.

"I'm listening," he told her.

Deanna offered him a small smile. She wasn't used to him being so unresponsive. And then, reaching out, she stroked his thigh. Maybe that would help him respond.

"I miss you, and I want things to go back to the way they were," she added in a voice that was sexy and flirtatious.

"Which is what, exactly?"

"You know," Deanna said, her fingers moving higher, toward his groin.

"To the friends-with-benefits arrangement?"

"It was working until I screwed things up."

Eric removed her hand from his leg, shaking his head as he did. "I can't believe this."

"I'm not trying to make light of things," Deanna said, realizing that her action may have come across that way. "I just—"

"Here I am, stupidly thinking that you started to let your wall down with me. That you were trusting me. That you were finally seeing we were good together. How stupid have I been?"

"I'm trying, Eric."

"Are you?" he challenged.

"Yes. It's not easy for me."

"Then why don't you start with the truth? Don't just tell me you're sorry for leaving me. Tell me why. Because one minute you were supposed to be making me breakfast, and the next I come out of the shower and you're gone."

Deanna was silent. In the car, the tension grew between them. It was as though they were in their own world, a bubble separated from the rest of reality. And part of her desperately wanted to flee, just as she had on Sunday.

"Tell me," Eric said.

"Brian," Deanna said softly, not meeting Eric's eyes. "Brian called."

"Again? When I was in the shower?"

"Yes. And he said the most horrible things. I was hurting, Eric. Suddenly doubting myself—"

"And you couldn't trust me with this? You had to run?"

"Trust…" Deanna's voice trailed off, and she sighed. "I gave my trust freely before. I was burned."

"So I have to pay for the mistakes of everyone else in your life?" Eric shot back.

"I trusted Mason."

"I'm not Mason."

"You have no idea how much what he did to me hurt—"

"I'm not Mason," Eric said more firmly.

"And to have your own mother not want you…"

"I'm not your mother."

"It's my fault, you know," Deanna said, finally meeting Eric's eyes head on. "Why my mother left."

Deanna hadn't expected those words to come from her lips, and apparently Eric hadn't, either, because he looked at her for a long moment, confusion on his face. Then he asked, "Why would you say that?"

Why indeed?

But suddenly…maybe it was doing the video appeal and now the news interview, but pieces were coming together in Deanna's mind in a way they hadn't before. "I don't know why I said that," Deanna said, noticing that her chest had gotten tight. "It's almost like I just remembered something. When I was young, I always felt that my mother left because of something I did. Not Callie or Natalie, but me. As I got older, I figured it was a typical child's guilt and tried to put it aside. Now, for whatever reason, that feeling has become even stronger over the last couple of days. I don't know what I could've done as a young child. And yet I still feel it's my fault. Something in my soul tells me it's my fault."

"You know that's not true," Eric said softly, reaching for her hand.

To feel his touch was amazing. Deanna sucked in a sharp breath and squeezed his hand in return.

"I'm sorry for the pain you're in," Eric said. "I really am."

Deanna sensed a "but" and quickly spoke. "Eric… I'm afraid."

"But leaving me the way you did—"

"You think it's easy? To tell you everything I've told you?"

"And haven't I proven to you that you can trust me with your fears and all your pain?" Eric challenged.

Deanna opened her mouth, but she said nothing. He was right. In her heart, she knew that. She knew that she trusted him implicitly, which was why she had dared to tell him what she had. Even the part about feeling that her mother had left because of her, a feeling that she didn't understand but one that was beginning to haunt her again. She felt comfortable sharing everything with Eric.

"But don't you get it?" she went on softly. "The very fact that I feel safe telling you all of this is also the very thing that scares me to death. Because I know that I need you in my life. And I'm terrified that if we cross the friendship line, something's going to get messed up between us. And I'm not going to have you in my life anymore—the guy I trusted wholeheartedly to be there for me and help me through my problems."

"You're doing a great job of pushing me away already—in case you haven't figured that out."

The words made Deanna's stomach clench. This was exactly what she had feared. Ruining things once she and Eric got involved sexually. She seemed to have an innate knack for messing up.

"Here's what I don't get," Eric went on. "I'm thinking the fact that you trust me so much shows that you do care about me. What better foundation for a relationship is there than that? Yet you let your fears stand in the way."

"It's not easy."

"Or maybe what you're saying is that I'm not worth it."

Deanna gaped at him. "No. Of course I'm not."

"You gave Marvin a chance. You gave Mason a chance.

Heck, you gave Brian a chance, and he sounds like a real class act."

"Eric—"

"And you push me away—the one guy who hasn't hurt you."

To hear him say it, she knew she sounded foolish. "I know it doesn't make sense. But maybe what's happening between us now is a result of us crossing the friendship line—the one thing I was most afraid of. Yes, I let those guys into my heart—and I got hurt. Maybe that's why my wall is up with you—because that's the only way to ensure that I don't lose you that same way. Don't you get it?"

Silence filled the air between them, so thick you could cut it. "So nice guys finish last," Eric said. "Again."

"That's not what I'm saying."

"Nice girls give themselves to bad boys all the time. Heck, as a principal, I see it even more. Yet I continue to be the nice guy. Why?"

It was a rhetorical question, more for himself, and Deanna didn't answer it.

"Maybe it will help to know that I'm not so nice, after all," Eric said.

"That's ridiculous, Eric."

"I've got my own secrets, Deanna. Secrets you might not like."

Deanna stared at him, at the firm set of his jaw and the resolved look in his eyes. And she realized that he was being entirely serious.

But she said, "I doubt that."

"You might feel differently once I'm done."

Deanna stared at him, confused. "What?"

"All those years ago, I knew that Marvin was seeing your sister. I knew he was seeing her before you ever came to tell me about it."

"What?" Deanna asked, her pulse beginning to accelerate.

"I knew. But I didn't tell you. And there was someone else, too. Someone else he was seeing while he was seeing you and your sister. And no, I'm not talking about Beverly."

Now Deanna gaped at him. "That's not true…"

"I was the nice guy. I debated telling you. But in the end, I wanted to spare you the humiliation. So I never told you. I regret that now. Maybe I should have. But a part of me knew that you needed to figure it out for yourself. And another part—the naive part—hoped that when you compared me to him, compared the jerk to his older brother who had been a constant friend and confidante, that the choice for you would be easy."

Deanna's lips were parted, but she didn't know what to say. "I… I…"

"After all these years, I have my answer," Eric said. "Nice guys just aren't your cup of tea."

"You knew about Marvin?" Deanna asked, and she wondered even as she did why she was worried about that part of what Eric had said to her. Why she was gripping those words like an armor to protect her.

Eric scoffed. "You say I don't get your issues, but you definitely don't understand what I'm trying to say. I'm not sure why I thought you would. But hey, at least now you can think of me as a jerk. Maybe that will actually give me a better shot with you."

Now Deanna's eyes narrowed. "That was a low blow."

"Deanna." Eric groaned. "I—"

"No, I get it." She quickly fumbled with the car door.

"Deanna, wait."

But she didn't. She quickly jumped out of the car and hurried toward the house, tears falling from her face.

Chapter 16

Eric pulled away from the curb at a rate of speed that caused his tires to burn. *Idiot, idiot, idiot!* he yelled to himself internally.

That was not what he planned to say. Not at all. But everything else he had tried to get through to Deanna had failed.

He had laid his heart on the line with her, told her how much he cared about her, that she could always trust him, and she still closed the door in his face.

That hurt. It hurt especially because he knew he would never hurt or betray her. And yet she had given her heart and her trust to men who had done just that time and time again.

Why wasn't he good enough?

That was the thought that plagued him as he came to a screeching halt at a stoplight. Two young girls who were crossing the street quickly jerked their heads in his direction in fright.

"Damn it, you've got to get a grip," Eric said to himself.

He was so angry, he almost went through a red light. And the consequences would have been catastrophic.

This wasn't him. He had never felt so out of control in his life. He'd never felt this kind of pain.

Except for when Deanna had headed for Hollywood nine years ago. Then, he had understood that she was so focused on Marvin that she couldn't see him in a romantic light. But now, he had told her how he felt, they had started a relationship and she was still rejecting him.

Rejecting him, yet he had been the one man who she had been able to trust all along.

The light turned green, and Eric began to drive again. He had fears, too—mostly that he would end up hurt because of her friends-with-benefits arrangement. But he had put his heart on the line for her nonetheless. The last thing he had wanted to do was hurt her with his words. They had been cruel—but they'd also been correct.

Because Deanna had given her heart to men who were not worthy of her, and here he was, a man who wanted nothing more than to adore her each day of his life, and she wouldn't let him in her heart.

Eric continued driving, with no particular destination in mind.

He found himself, an hour later, at the neighborhood bar he used to frequent with Hector, a place where they would get together to shoot pool and shoot the breeze.

He'd called Hector, whom he hadn't hung out with in a while, and he agreed to meet Eric there. Hector had always told Eric that he was foolish for maintaining his hopeful romanticism. That he needed to get with the program just like all the other guys on the planet and take what women so freely offered without a care.

He needed to see Hector now, to help him get his head out of the clouds where Deanna was concerned.

"I told you, man," Hector said now. They were sitting side-by-side at the bar. "You play the nice guy, women don't appreciate that. Sure, they'll cry on your shoulder. Complain about the men they're really into…"

Eric fiddled with his beer bottle. Unfortunately, Hector's words were true. Eric had always been that guy—the one there for the girl—and yet he was the one suffering rejection.

"It's time for you be a different kind of man. A different kind of cat. Girls don't like nice. No matter what they say."

Eric took a swig of his beer. He was on his second bottle. This wasn't exactly like him, but this was a day from hell. He couldn't go back to being Deanna's friend. He wanted all or nothing.

And he knew there would be no *all*. Because after he had given all he had to give, Eric knew she would never love him.

"I'm hearing you, Hector. Took me a long time, but I'm hearing you."

Hector clamped a hand down on his shoulder. He was attractive, part Hispanic and part African-American, and had a smile that made women putty in his hands. "That's my man," Hector said.

Eric knew he was playing a part. The part of the angry man ready to take revenge in another woman's bed. But he needed to vent, that was all.

Hector looked in the direction of two women who were at the end of the bar, smiling flirtatiously in their direction. "This is your chance, man. Go with it. See how it feels to just be a man who takes what he wants."

The problem was, Eric didn't want that. He didn't want whatever those women were offering.

He had only engaged in a friends-with-benefits relationship with Deanna because he cared deeply for her, not because he wanted casual sex.

"I think the taller one likes you," Hector said.

Eric looked in their direction. Indeed, the taller woman was definitely making eye contact with him. And she seemed to be getting encouragement from her friend to approach him, if the not-so-subtle arm nudging was any indication.

"She's coming," Hector said, lightly punching Eric on the shoulder.

She *was* coming. Walking toward him with an exaggerated hip-swaying movement. Flawless dark skin, bright eyes, an hourglass figure—she was undoubtedly a beautiful woman. But even before she reached him, Eric found himself rising from the stool and turning toward the door.

"Hey?" Hector called, confusion in his voice.

Eric headed for the front door without stopping. This wasn't his scene.

And most important, that woman was not Deanna.

And Deanna was the only one he wanted.

Two days later, Deanna was at Callie's place, suffering what sure felt like a broken heart. Despite all her talk about protecting herself by not getting emotionally involved, she was hurting.

She had called the school and told them she wasn't feeling well and wouldn't be able make the rehearsal. There was no way she could face Eric. So she was with Callie now, trying to distract herself from her feelings by discussing the updates regarding the search for their mother. There had been several calls already—emails, too—all of which were looking like false leads.

"It's as I feared," Callie said. "Every freak and their dog has been calling the police hotline, claiming they have information regarding our mother. But it's to be expected. The problem is that it's going to take the police a long time to go through all of the potential leads."

"Yeah, I'm sure. But we still have to keep the faith that we're going to get the right lead."

"Which is what I keep telling Natalie. But she's pretty upset. I guess she expected that we'd have heard from our mother by now."

"I know," Deanna said. "That's Natalie. She tries so hard to be optimistic that when things don't go the way she hopes, she can get pretty unhappy."

"She's not the only one who's unhappy," Callie said, giving her a pointed look. "I mean, you should just call him."

"It's not that easy."

"Pick up the phone. Punch in his number. Or better yet, head to his place."

"We can't go back," Deanna said. "Things were said… it was ugly."

"Things you both needed to hash out," Callie stressed.

Deanna rested her cheek in her palm, feeling totally deflated as she remembered the ugly exchange with Eric in his SUV. She'd worried herself endlessly about how she couldn't stand the idea of losing their friendship. And now, that was exactly what had happened.

"Friends with benefits was never going to work. Not for you and Eric. He loves you, Deanna."

"I'm not so sure."

"You know what I am sure of?" Callie asked. "That you love him."

Deanna's eyes flew to hers. "Wh-what?"

"Seriously," Callie went on. "I don't remember seeing you this upset. Ever."

Deanna's stomach lurched, and her heart felt as though someone had squeezed it in a vise. She was hurting. No doubt about it. But love?

She only knew that she was feeling deeper pain than she had known in a long, long time.

"I can't believe he knew that Marvin was cheating and he never told me," Deanna said.

Callie looked at her sister in dismay. "Please tell me you're joking. That can't be what you're concerned about."

"It's just…" Deanna began and stopped. Her brain knew she was being irrational, but her heart… "Knowing that he knew and didn't tell me…I feel like a bigger fool."

Callie made a face as she looked at her sister. "Seems to me you're looking for reasons to be upset with him. Certainly you can't blame him for what happened. He's not the one at fault. And it sounds as though he really cared about you— enough to protect you from Marvin's bad behavior."

"Which he would have accomplished had he told me," Deanna insisted.

"Maybe. Maybe not. But you're forgetting one critical part of this. Your sister was involved with your man. What do you think Eric felt about that? That he should tell you what had happened and totally destroy your relationship with Natalie? Think about his predicament."

Deanna said nothing.

"I love you, sis. But you're doing the same thing I did for a while. Making excuses to run. All I can say is that it sounds as though Eric has been nothing but thoughtful and considerate."

The fight was gone out of her. Deanna knew that her sister was right. For some reason, she simply wanted to hold on to an excuse to be angry with Eric.

"I guess the truth is…I'm afraid." She stifled sob. "What if I call him and he still wants nothing to do with me? Maybe he needs more time."

"You won't know until you try."

"I was so afraid that this day would come," Deanna said, more to herself. "When Eric wouldn't want to talk to me anymore. And now it's here. I'm the one who told him I wanted to go back to being friends, so why do I feel this awful?"

Callie rose from the armchair and sat beside Deanna on the sofa. She put her arm around her. "It's not that hard to understand, Deanna. You're in love."

This time, when Deanna heard her sister's words, they truly registered. And this time, she didn't immediately tell herself that the words couldn't be true.

Instead, she allowed the barrier that she was so used to keeping up to slip down.

And that's when the reality hit her and she realized the utter truth at her core.

She *was* in love with Eric.

"You want to control everything. Protect your heart. You think I don't know what that's like?" Callie asked gently. "Didn't I do the same thing? I guess it's clear we're definitely sisters," she added, hugging Deanna a little tighter.

"Eric loves you, Deanna," said Callie. "That much is as clear as day. And if you're like me, you're pushing him away because you think that's going to protect you in the long run. Sorry to burst your bubble, sis, but it's not."

Deanna drew in a shaky breath. Her sister was right. Somehow, she had needed to hear these words from Callie's mouth. Or maybe she'd simply needed the time and this painful experience of losing Eric to realize what mattered most to her.

Because the other guys she had loved and lost were a blip on the radar in comparison to what she felt knowing that she might have lost Eric forever.

The only thing worse for her had been losing her mother. Even Mason's betrayal paled in comparison to what she was feeling now, knowing that she had pushed the one man who had always been there for her out of her life.

"What do I do?" Deanna asked her sister. "How do I make this right?"

"You make a compelling argument. You were able to push him away even though you love him. I'm sure with a little effort you can also make a compelling argument to win him back."

Callie flashed an encouraging smile. "Deanna, if he loves you, and I know he does, then you'll get past this. He'll understand where your fear is coming from. If Nigel could forgive me for keeping his son from him for nine years, Eric can forgive you. We Hart women may say one thing, but I think it's pretty obvious to the guys in our lives what's in our hearts. That's why they forgive us. Despite what we say, they know better."

Callie's words uplifted Deanna. She was absolutely right. Given her own experience with Nigel, Callie clearly understood Deanna's fears when it came to love. Not to mention the shared experience of being abandoned by their mother, which had affected all of the Hart sisters.

But the fact that Callie and Nigel had worked it out despite huge obstacles proved that Deanna could work it out, too. Callie was happy. She was a changed woman from the person Deanna had seen that day she had arrived for their aunt's funeral. Now that she had made peace with Nigel, she was on cloud nine. She was living the life she had meant to live ten years earlier.

Even Natalie had faced her fears. How hard was it to go on when the man you'd married had made a fool of you in the public? Yet it was only when Natalie had stopped fighting Michael's love and allowed herself to be open to the possibility that she had once again found happiness.

Her sisters had done it. She could do it, too.

Deanna slipped her arms around Callie and hugged her tightly. "I needed this. Your talk has completely made me put things into perspective. It's so obvious to me that I have never felt this devastated at the idea of losing someone—ever." She got to her feet. "I just hope that it's not too late."

Chapter 17

Deanna left her sister's place with a mission in mind. The mission—to not sabotage herself and her relationships ever again.

No, not relationships. *Relationship.* With Eric. Because he was the only man she wanted.

Perhaps she had always wanted him. She certainly knew that turning to him was the one thing that made her feel comforted. She had trusted him with her problems over and over again. Connecting the dots now, she could see that she had trusted him with her problems because she knew she could trust him with her heart.

She had just been so afraid of losing him. So afraid that she had caused the very thing she had feared.

But she was not going to live with that fear anymore. Now, she was going to do whatever it took to make him understand that she was in it for the long haul.

But when she went to Eric's house, she didn't find him there.

She went back to her car, where she decided she would wait for him. He had to show up sometime.

As she waited, her phone made a little musical sound, indicating that she had an email. Eric, she thought, and quickly checked to see what the message was.

She couldn't have been more surprised when she discovered that it was an email sent to her website account, with the heading I KNEW YOUR MOTHER. PLEASE CALL ME.

Deanna quickly opened the message and read.

Deanna, I saw your plea on television with your sisters, and you can't imagine how happy I was to see your face. You and your sisters.

It's been a very long time since I've seen you. I left a message on the police hotline but haven't heard back. That's why I'm reaching out to you.

I'm your grandfather, Deanna. And I'm here in Cleveland. I came as soon as I saw your story. Please call me at 404-555-9833. I have information about your mother. We need to talk as soon as possible. We can meet at a coffee shop so that you can determine for yourself.

Deanna was stunned as she finished reading the words. In fact, she reread them.

Could this be true? Her grandfather?

An Atlanta area code.

Her heart filled with hope. And hadn't Callie told her that the police were sifting through tons of leads? The fact that this person had mentioned calling the police hotline but not hearing back made sense. She felt it in her gut.

Yes, this is it.

But there had been so many false leads. So she would call this person, meet with him. She would vet this person first before contacting her sisters, ask the critical questions to determine whether the person was the real deal. No point getting Natalie's and Callie's hopes up only to be disappointed once again.

Deanna punched in the number the man had given, realizing that he hadn't even mentioned his name. The phone rang once, twice, then a third time.

Just as Deanna thought it would go to voice mail, someone picked up.

"Hello?"

The man that answered the phone was clearly older, and for whatever reason, that gave Deanna hope.

"Um, hi," she said. "You sent me an email message. About—"

"Your mother," the man supplied, and Deanna could hear a smile in his voice. "Deanna?"

"Yes," she said, guarded.

"My name is Calvin. Calvin Harrison. Your older sister, Callie, got her name in my honor. At least that's what your mother said."

Oh, my God. Deanna was even more certain now, but she couldn't be sure. Not until she met him. "You said you have information about my mother?" Deanna said

"Yes. Mary. I knew her as Mary Harrison in Atlanta. You called her Miriam Hart on the news, but you and your sisters, I would know you anywhere. You're my kin."

Deanna didn't want to get too hopeful, but even this fit with the story. She and her sisters believed their mother had likely used a different name, at least at one point in her life.

She would meet with Calvin, figure out exactly who he was and report back to her sisters if she believed that he was indeed their grandfather. "When can we meet?"

"I'm free right now. I'm staying at a hotel downtown. On East Ninth Street at Superior." He told her the name of the popular hotel chain. "Do you know it?"

"Yes. Yes, I do."

"Across the street, there's a coffee shop, a place named Betty's."

"Yes, I know it. How about I meet you there?"

"Certainly. I can head there now."

"I'll need about twenty minutes," Deanna told him. "How will I know you?"

"I'm wearing a blue shirt with tan khaki pants," he said. "I'm seventy-two years old. You'll know me. I'll be the man with the huge smile on his face when he sees his granddaughter enter the coffee shop."

Eric didn't arrive in the next few minutes, so Deanna made her way downtown and to Betty's. She was nervous but cautiously optimistic. Everything about her brief chat with Calvin told her that he was legit. He had mentioned Atlanta, she hadn't. Plus, he was seventy-two years old. It didn't stand to reason that a seventy-two-year-old man would have headed here from Atlanta on a whim.

No, he'd heard their story and had recognized it. Recognized it because it was his story.

Deanna found a parking spot and then walked down the street to the coffee shop where Calvin would be waiting. And when she stepped inside the establishment, her eyes darted around anxiously. After no more than a few seconds of looking she saw the man she knew was related to her. A wide smile erupted on his face, and he got to his feet instantly.

"Deanna," he said.

Deanna moved toward him, her smile growing with each of her steps. And then she stopped in front of him, tentative. She still wanted to keep this strictly business until she got the answers she needed.

But when Calvin opened his arms to her, Deanna found herself walking into his embrace.

He hugged her heartily and she could hear the emotion in

his voice as he drew in a relieved breath. "Deanna, it's really you. After all this time."

They pulled apart, and Deanna was aware that people were regarding them with curiosity.

"Please, sit," Calvin said, and she did.

"I took the liberty of ordering you some lemonade. You used to really like that, when you were young. You used to love the lemonade your grandmother made for you."

"I did?"

Calvin nodded. "You sure did."

Deanna said nothing as she stared at him, her eyes taking in his every feature. His nose was hers, no doubt about it. And she had his cheekbones. And she could see bits of her sisters in his face, as well.

This man was a relative of hers. Absolutely.

"Where's my mother?" Deanna asked.

"Well, that's the thing. It's a long story. But I'll tell you everything. I'll start from the beginning."

Deanna took a sip of her lemonade. "Please."

Deanna regarded Calvin, waited for him to speak. But first, he sipped his lemonade. Then he raised a glass almost as if in salute. "This is fine lemonade, don't you think? Almost as good as your grandmother used to make."

Deanna nodded and took another sip. "It's delicious."

"But I suppose that's not what you want to hear about. You asked about your mother."

"I hope you're not offended at the way I asked." She wondered now if she'd sounded too brusque. "It's just that you heard our plea, and my sisters and I are desperate to find our mother. But that doesn't mean that I'm not happy to meet you, as well. I guess I'm just a little flustered. And a lot overwhelmed. As much as I hoped that this day would come, I didn't really know that it would. It's been twenty-three years since I saw my mother. Can you believe it?"

"The last I saw you was twenty-four years ago. In Atlanta. Do you remember me at all?" He looked at her, his eyes searching, saying that he hoped she would remember something.

"I'm sorry," Deanna said honestly. "I wish I did remember. But…that was such a long time ago. I was only five or six."

"So you have no memory of what happened in Georgia?"

If Deanna had needed further proof that this man was indeed a relative, his question solidified it. Something had happened in Georgia. Her mother had gone back there to take care of unfinished business, as she had claimed to Ms. Dottie in Philadelphia.

"No. I don't know what happened."

Calvin glanced around nervously and then leaned forward. He spoke in a low tone. "You don't remember that night? At all?"

And then Deanna felt a jolt. And something flashed in her brain. Something that left her with the same unsettling feeling she had when she'd dreamed about the man abusing the woman. Brian abusing her.

Calvin's eyes widened slightly. "You do? You do remember?"

"No." Deanna shook her head. "I don't. I've just been having strange dreams. Dreams that I was certain had to do with an ex-boyfriend of mine. He was abusive to me. But that's another story that I won't get into now." She paused briefly. "The thing is, every so often I get the feeling that my dreams are not about him and me but about other people. Which doesn't make any sense."

Calvin sighed softly, and Deanna could tell that there was a story there.

"Whatever it is, you can tell me," she said. "I know that something really bad must have happened in Georgia. If my mother did something horrible, or something horrible happened to her, you have to tell me."

Calvin nodded. "I suppose I should just get to it. I should also tell you this—I don't know where your mother is. But I came here knowing that I had to reconnect with my granddaughters. I hope you don't mind."

"No," Deanna said. But she couldn't help being a little bit disappointed.

"Maybe together we can find her," Calvin suggested. "Are you absolutely certain you have no idea where she is?"

"Definitely certain." Deanna made a face. "It's the whole reason we went to the media."

"Perhaps you never will, then," Calvin said, shaking his head with a remorseful expression on his face.

"Why would you say that?"

"Because of what she did. Because of what she did that night. The last night I saw you and your sisters."

Chapter 18

Deanna stared at Calvin, wanting him to elaborate. But again, he glanced around nervously, clearly concerned about being overheard. So she said, "Why don't we head outside? There are a couple of benches on the street. We can sit there and talk. Have more privacy."

"Yes. That's a good idea. It's a pleasant day. We can sip our lemonade out there."

"Exactly. And most importantly, we'll have no prying ears for whatever it is that you want to tell me." Because Deanna could tell that whatever he had to say was significant. She could almost feel his fear as he gazed around uncomfortably.

They exited the coffee shop and walked the short distance to an available bench. Calvin sat first, and Deanna sat beside him. She wasn't certain, but he seemed to look more frail now than when he had first stood up to greet her. Perhaps the weight of whatever he was about to tell her was getting to him.

"Whatever it is," Deanna began, "I can handle it."

"Your mother," Calvin began, and then he stopped. His eyes actually misted with tears. "Your mother. She left Georgia. She left me. She left all of us. Because something horrible happened. I don't want you to judge her harshly. But we didn't always get along. She and her sister—"

"Auntie Jean," Deanna supplied.

"Yes. Jean. Mary and Jean were both a bit of a handful. They left one day, teenagers thinking they could take on the world. Broke your grandmother's heart, I tell you. We always thought they'd come back. When Mary did come back, years later, she had three kids in tow. She told us how the father of her children had been killed in an accident and she was having some hard times. Mostly, she said she felt guilty for walking away from us without so much as a backward glance. You can imagine how elated your grandmother was to see her. As was I. This was my daughter. We didn't care what she'd done. We loved her. But I knew things weren't right with her. I always got the sense that she was running with the wrong crowd, that she'd been in some sort of trouble she didn't want to tell us about. And I don't know what happened with Jean, but we never saw her again." He paused, exhaled sharply.

Deanna said, "Go on."

"Then came that night. I don't remember how the argument started. I think your grandmother was upset with your mother because of something we learned about one of her boyfriends. The guy was no good, a criminal. We were concerned for Mary, for you children. But your mother took offense to what we had to say. Felt we were putting her down for her choices, when we were just trying to look out for you. I never judged her for whatever she'd gotten into. I loved her then and I love her still. But I couldn't just stand by and let her put you children in harm's way."

Deanna wasn't sure she even took one breath as she listened to her grandfather tell his story.

"As I said, I don't remember how the argument started," he went on. "But all I know is that we talked to your mother about keeping you children with us. She didn't like the suggestion. Not one bit." Calvin paused, then inhaled an audible breath. "She—she had a gun."

Deanna gasped. "What?"

"I'm sure it was an accident. And maybe the fact that she'd been drinking, or maybe she was even stoned, I don't know… Said she'd shoot us if we didn't let her take you kids."

Deanna squeezed her eyes tight, and she saw a flash of light. Before, she had always assumed that that flash of light was simply a jolt of discomfort at a painful memory. But now, she had to wonder if she was remembering the flash of a gunshot going off in a darkened room.

Her eyes popped open. She saw Calvin staring at her with concern.

"You remember," he said.

Deanna shook her head. "No. Not really. But…but I feel the memory is there. It's within my grasp."

And it suddenly hit her. The dreams she'd been having after the incident with Brian had nothing to do with her and Brian at all. It was a memory of something else. A memory that had been brought back to the surface because of Brian's abuse.

"You saw it, child. It was you. My middle grandchild. You saw the gun go off. I saw you standing there. You were scared as anything. And I grabbed you, I tried to protect you."

A man and woman struggling. Her grandfather and her mother? He had been trying to protect her from her mother?

"What are you saying?" Deanna asked. She needed to know exactly what had happened.

"Your grandmother was shot that night," Calvin explained.

Deanna gasped in horror. And then her lungs constricted. She could hardly take in air.

"Your grandmother was shot," Calvin went on, and his voice caught in his throat. "God rest her soul. I know your mother didn't mean it. But it happened, and she left. And that was the last I saw of her, of you. I tried to find her. But obviously, she changed her name. She didn't want to be found. She didn't want to go to jail for what she'd done. What she didn't understand was that I had forgiven her. When you love your child, you'll forgive them for anything."

Tears were streaming down Deanna's face. Her mother had killed her grandmother? That was why she had run from Georgia? Had Auntie Jean known?

This was excruciatingly painful. Deanna didn't want to believe it could be true, but she knew that her mother had been involved with some criminals. Had she had a drug or alcohol addiction that had fueled her violent behavior that night?

"I…I can't believe it."

"I'm telling you this so you understand what happened. You also have to understand that your mother was out of her mind. When people are high on drugs, they can't see straight. They don't know what they're doing. It's why I had to forgive her. As much as I missed your grandmother, I had to forgive your mom because I knew that she didn't know what she was doing."

Waves of devastation rolled over Deanna. All this time, she'd been looking for her mother, fearing that something awful had happened to her. And now, it appeared that her mother had been running because she wanted to escape justice.

No wonder she had not come back for them. No wonder she had not wanted to have anything to do with them. She'd been on the run all this time, looking over her shoulder at every turn.

Because she'd killed her own mother.

Did it really matter how it had happened? Tragic incidents like that were born of bad decisions and bad behavior.

Oh, the years of pain her grandfather must have endured because of what her mother had done!

Deanna shot to her feet. She felt unsteady and drew in a deep breath.

She couldn't help the tears. She had her answers, but they were not what she would have ever prayed for. Not in a million years.

"I—I have to go." She drank off half of her lemonade in almost one gulp, needing something to quench her thirst. Something to distract her from the news she had heard.

Her mother was a killer.

And as much a she had never expected that she would ever think this in her life, she found herself wishing that she didn't know. She found herself wishing that she and her sisters never got the answers they had so desperately sought. Because some things in life were better off left secret.

"I'm so sorry," Calvin said as he stood beside her. "Do you want to come to my hotel room? It's just across the street, we can continue talking there. You look like you should maybe lie down."

Deanna shook her head fervently. "No," she said. "I'm fine. I have to talk to my sisters." She started to walk in one direction, then realized that her car was in the opposite direction. Then she stopped, realizing that she was about to walk off and leave Calvin without a goodbye.

She was so unsettled, so frazzled from what she had learned. "Calvin—or should I call you Grandfather? I'm so sorry."

"Child, it's not for you to be sorry. It wasn't your fault."

Perhaps not, but shouldn't she have remembered? She had witnessed this horrible incident. She closed her eyes, saw the muzzle flash in the darkened room. The man and woman struggling.

She moaned softly. Something about the image in her mind still bothered her.

Of course it would bother her. Her mother fighting with her grandfather. He was lucky to have escaped unscathed.

"I have your number. I know your hotel. I've got to go see my sisters." Her breathing was coming in sharp gasps, and she could hardly form a coherent thought.

My mother is a murderer...

"They'll want to talk to you for sure. And Nigel. That's my brother-in-law to-be. He's a police officer. I'm sure he's gonna want to talk to you, too."

Deanna's head began to throb. She paced two steps in one direction and then two steps in the other direction. Sheesh, she felt like a caged animal, wild with anger and ready to tear apart the barriers holding her back.

"I have to go. I'm sorry."

And flustered, she headed off to her car. She fumbled with the keys, and it was several seconds before she could get in. She looked over her shoulder and saw that Calvin was standing there, looking concerned. She got behind the wheel of the car and started it as fast as she could. And then she slammed her foot on the gas and burst off into traffic.

She heard a horn blare. Clearly she had just cut someone off. But she couldn't think about that.

My mother is a murderer...

She drove. She cried. With each mile she went, her head was feeling heavier and heavier. Heavy with the distress of knowing the truth.

But then her arms began to feel heavy, as well. Everything about her suddenly felt as though she were floating, not really there. As though a haze had come down over her.

Deanna felt the car jerk a nanosecond before she heard the

crashing sound. Panic gripped her as she tried to make sense of what was going on. The last thing she remembered was the sensation of spinning, of not being able to control the car.

And then everything went black.

Chapter 19

Eric returned home late, after spending a solid two hours at the gym. He had stayed at the school later than he normally would, hoping that despite Deanna calling in to say she was too ill to be at the rehearsal, she would show up nonetheless.

But she hadn't.

Eric hadn't wanted to go back to his house. Suddenly, it didn't seem the same without Deanna. He had lived there for years, and yet in over a month's time she had indelibly left her mark on the place.

He loved her. He knew that. But he also knew that the ball was in her court. Hopefully the day would soon come when she realized that he was a good man, one who would never hurt her, and she would be able to embrace him. But he couldn't persuade her to come to that conclusion. She had to make that determination for herself.

Every part of him believed that she would. Unless he was completely delusional, what they had shared together as they'd made love countless times could not be faked. It wasn't simply about feeling good. Not simply about giving and receiving carnal pleasure. Yes, there had been pleasure, but there had been so much more.

Eric was never in the least bit interested in sex without the strings, because he believed there was more brewing between him and Deanna than friendship. It had been brewing nine years ago. And with every touch, every sigh, every gaze into his eyes, she was telling him that she loved him.

Some women were like a delicate flower. They needed time to bloom. Deanna needed time to bloom.

She needed time to bloom and realize that she was beautiful, worthy and not to blame for all the bad things that had happened to her. Eric fully believed in his heart that when she let the pain go, she would be able to receive the love he was offering.

Though trying to remain positive while giving Deanna her space, he still felt glum. As he entered his house, Sadie greeted him at the door, but seeing his cat only marginally lifted his mood. Two days without talking to Deanna was two days too long. Already, it felt as if they'd been apart for a year.

Eric turned on the television and sank onto his sofa. He'd already picked up fast food, which he had eaten in his car. He hadn't felt like cooking a meal at home, not when all he could remember was how he and Deanna had laughed in the kitchen while preparing a meal together.

He had to put her out of his mind, at least for now, or he would go crazy. So he changed the channel until he got to a local news station.

He couldn't have been more surprised, when, a couple of minutes later, a picture of Deanna appeared in the corner of the screen. A blonde female news reporter stood at the scene of a car crash.

Eric's heart leaped into his throat. Good God, what had happened?

The volume had been down, as Eric had mostly been watching the screen as a distraction. Now, he quickly turned it up.

"...witnesses say they aren't sure what happened, only that Deanna Hart was driving erratically before the crash. As for the extent of her injuries, we aren't sure yet. She was unconscious when paramedics arrived, but she had a pulse. She's been rushed to Fairview Hospital, and we're awaiting word on her condition."

Unconscious. Not sure of the extent of her injuries. Eric's heart nearly stopped.

"You will remember that just days ago, Deanna Hart, along with her sisters, made a plea for their mother's return," the reporter continued. "This is certainly a sad and bizarre turn of events."

"We'll be praying for her," the female anchor at the news desk said when the screen went to her in the newsroom.

Eric was already on his feet. And as he ran out the door, the fallacy of his thoughts hit him in the face. He had thought that all Deanna needed was time. Time to figure out that she wanted to be with him.

But based on what he'd seen on the news, the sad reality was she might not have any time left.

"Oh, Eric—thank God you're here."

Callie immediately enveloped Eric in a hug and held him tightly for several seconds. They were in the emergency room waiting area, as opposed to a room with Deanna, which caused Eric more concern.

Pulling apart, he asked, "How is she?"

Callie wiped at tears. "Thank the Lord, she's going to be okay."

"I saw the story on the news. They said she was unconscious on the scene."

"Mmm-hmm," Callie concurred. "They rushed her here, fearful that she had a serious head injury because she was unresponsive. She regained consciousness once she got here, but she was completely out of it, talking gibberish, and the doctors in the trauma unit feared she had a bad concussion, or worse. But tests showed no swelling in the brain—at least not so far. Based on some witness reports about her driving erratically, they did blood tests. That's when they discovered that she was unresponsive because she'd ingested a date rape drug."

"What? I don't understand," Eric exclaimed.

"Neither do we," Callie said. "She was at my place, then she left to see you. The next thing, I'm getting a call that she's in the hospital."

"Wait—she was going to see me?"

"Yeah. She left my place around five."

Dear God, no. Deanna had gone to his place—and he hadn't been there.

Guilt washed over Eric. If he had only been home, would Deanna be in this situation right now?

He glanced around the waiting room. Natalie was inconsolable, but Michael was comforting her. Callie had wandered back over to Nigel, who was standing near Michael and Natalie.

Nigel was the one that Eric wanted to speak to. He was a police officer and certainly had to know more about what was going on than anyone else in the room.

"Nigel," Eric said when he reached him. "What happened? Besides the crash. I want to know how this happened, and why."

"There's a lot going on," Nigel said. "A lot we're not sure about."

"But you must know something," Eric challenged. "Something that hasn't been publicized in the media."

Nigel pursed his lips.

"Tell me," Eric insisted.

"All we know is that Deanna met with a man named Calvin Harrison. They were seen on a surveillance tape together at a coffee shop. Calvin was seen checking into a hotel. And shortly after, witnesses say they saw Calvin and Deanna part, and Calvin returned to his hotel and checked out. We found an email that was open on Deanna's phone, with this man's name and number. He identified himself as her grandfather, which explains why she met him. But we've called his number, and he's not picking up."

Eric nodded. Then he asked, "What else?"

"My colleagues have done some digging," Nigel told him. "This Calvin Harrison character has a criminal record. So we're not feeling too confident about the fact that the timing of the accident and his appearance in town were coincidental. It's seeming very likely that he's the one who drugged her."

"So is he really her grandfather…?" Eric asked, aghast.

"We don't know, but if he met her and drugged her, that means he set her up. That his goal was to kill her."

The day's turns of event were baffling, but everyone's attention turned to Deanna once they were allowed to visit her.

Walking into the room and seeing the woman he loved stretched out on a hospital bed, with tubes attached to her and blinking, beeping monitors, Eric was barely able to stand it. He wanted to ball his hands into fists and scream at the top of his lungs.

He loved this woman, and someone had damn near killed her.

Eric didn't leave Deanna's side. He held vigil at the hospital with her sisters and her uncle until she awoke from the painkillers and other drugs the doctors had administered. Only when she had been able to look around the room and recognize everyone did Eric believe that she would be okay.

"Eric," she said softly.

He gripped her hands. "Yes, I'm here. I'm here, Deanna."

Her lips curled in the faintest of smiles.

"I love you," Eric went on. "I always have, and I always will." He kissed the top of her hand.

She didn't respond, but that was okay. Eric knew that she'd heard him, and that was the most important thing.

Later, when the hospital staff told him that only immediate family members would be allowed to stay the night, he made it clear that he wasn't going anywhere. He planted himself in a chair at her side, and no one was going to make him leave. There was no way he was going to be able to go home and get any sleep, not when the woman he loved was lying here in a hospital bed, put here at the hands of a man who was her grandfather.

What was going on? Why would Deanna's own grandfather want to kill her?

Eric watched the news that night, where there was more about the story. The details about the GHB having been found in Deanna's blood and the fact that she'd met with a man named Calvin Harrison were released. Eric watched the report with a sense of disbelief. It felt surreal, as if it couldn't possibly be true. And yet Deanna lay in a hospital bed, clear proof that evil existed in the world.

Eric should have been home when she had come by. He should have been there for her. If he had, she likely wouldn't be in this hospital bed right now. Because he would have gone with her to meet Calvin. He would have made sure that nothing had happened to her.

Had anything worse happened to Deanna, Eric would never have been able to forgive himself.

All he knew was that when Deanna got out of the hospital, Eric would hold on to her and never let her go.

Chapter 20

Deanna was released from the hospital the next day, after further tests proved she didn't have more than a mild concussion. With the GHB out of her system, she was sent home with painkillers for any residual pain from the bump on her head and any other discomfort from the crash.

She was groggy, but as Eric drove her home, Deanna reached for his hand. "Eric," she said, her voice hoarse with emotion. "I'm so sorry. Everything I said to you, I didn't mean it. I was just scared."

"Shh. It's okay. We'll talk later."

He saw her to her uncle's house, where the sofa bed in the living room was ready for her, that way she wouldn't have to travel up and down a set of stairs. Eric helped her into the bed, where her sisters, uncle and nephew immediately surrounded her.

Eric sat on a nearby recliner. He watched Deanna drift off to sleep.

And then sleep claimed him, as well.

* * *

Eric didn't realize he had drifted off to sleep until his eyes popped open. After an instant of confusion, he realized that he was no longer at the hospital but in Deanna's home. He hadn't slept much the night in the hospital, instead forcing himself to stay awake to help monitor her condition. No wonder he'd fallen asleep now.

As his eyes settled on Deanna, it broke his heart to see her curled up on the sofa bed, looking weak. He got up and approached her and was rewarded with a smile.

"Hey," she said softly.

"Hey," Eric returned, sitting beside her on the bed.

Callie took Kwame and led him out of the room, no doubt to give them privacy.

"You were sleeping for a while," Deanna said softly.

"I guess I couldn't keep my eyes open anymore."

"You haven't left me," she went on, her voice holding a hint of wonder.

"And I'm not going to."

"I really am sorry," she told him. "Everything I said to you, the way I pushed you away…I was so stupid."

"It's okay." Eric took her hand in his, and kissed it. "I know what you were doing. And that's why I'm here. I'm not going anywhere. I pressed you about what our relationship was, but I shouldn't have. In my heart, I knew what we had. I didn't need to hear you say it."

"Yes, you did," Deanna said softly. "You deserved to hear me say that we were more than just friends with benefits. I don't know why it was so hard for me to say what I already knew in my soul. You're perfect for me, Eric. I think I knew that even nine years ago…I just…I just couldn't trust in love." She paused, held his gaze. "But I do now. And if I'd died before I could tell you this…" Her voice cracked.

"Hey, it's okay. You're fine. And no one is going to hurt you again. Not while I'm here to do something about it."

"I love you, Eric," Deanna told him. "I'm in love with you."

A smile erupted on Eric's face as the warmest feeling spread through his body. Deanna's eyes, however, filled with tears. "It's okay, baby. I love you, too. You know that."

Eric brought his hand to her face to gently wipe away the tears. "Thank you," Deanna said. "Thank you for loving me. For not giving up on me."

"I could no more give up on you than I could willingly stop breathing."

"I don't know why he came after me," Deanna said. "My own grandfather. Why would he want to hurt me?"

"The police are going to track him down," Eric assured her. "You rest. Don't worry about him." He sat with her, brushing her forehead affectionately as her eyes fluttered shut. He wouldn't leave her side. He was here with her, through thick and thin, for better or for worse. He didn't need to take a vow to love her forever to know that he would do just that.

After short while later, the doorbell rang, and Deanna's eyes flew open.

Eric looked over his shoulder, wondering who could be at the door when everybody who cared about Deanna was here in this room.

"You think it's a reporter?" Natalie asked. "You think they figured out Deanna's here, not at Michael's place?"

The sisters had come up with the plan to leak false news that Deanna would be recuperating in Michael's home, so that their uncle's quiet street would not be disrupted with news vans. And so far, it was working. Michael had confirmed that reporters were camped outside of his house, waiting for a sighting of Deanna. Once Deanna had been safely tucked away in the home, the family had moved their cars to other streets and come into the yard through the alley in the back.

"I don't see any reporters outside," Kwame said, peering through the blinds in the front window.

"One of them may have figured it out," Callie said. "We're not going to be rid of the media anytime soon."

That was for sure. With Deanna's celebrity status, as well as Natalie's and Michael's, people were interested in the Hart sisters as though they knew them. Add to that the salacious nature of this story, and it stood to reason that the media would hound the sisters. Given that the police believed Calvin Harrison had deliberately drugged his granddaughter, they didn't believe the story that he'd told Deanna about her mother being a killer. Rather, they believed Calvin had targeted Deanna, but they didn't know why.

"I'll get rid of whoever it is," Callie said.

Eric faced Deanna again, stroked her forehead.

For a moment there was silence, then Callie gasped and uttered, "Oh, God!"

Eric whirled to face her, his adrenaline racing, fearing he was about to see Calvin Harrison standing in the room. Instead, he witnessed Natalie covering her mouth with both hands.

Slowly, a woman stepped forward. And seeing the person, Deanna gripped Eric's hand. Hard.

And despite her injuries, Deanna sat up. Eric noticed her hand was trembling.

"Mom?" Natalie said, her voice shaky with emotion.

And then Eric understood.

Deanna's mother had returned.

Natalie surged forward, immediately throwing her arms around her mother. Callie stood transfixed, as though she couldn't believe what she was seeing. Nigel stepped up behind Callie and placed his hands on her shoulders.

"Mom?" Deanna asked, now lowering her feet to the floor.

Certainly she wasn't dreaming. She wasn't hallucinating because of the pain medication.

Her mother looked in her direction then—and oh, that face! All doubt was erased from Deanna's mind. Her face was drawn, and she looked older than a woman in her early fifties, but those high cheekbones and wide eyes—the same features Deanna saw when she looked in the mirror every day—solidified for her that indeed, their mother was truly here.

"My, baby," Miriam said. And without waiting for an invitation, she moved toward Deanna with quick steps. She reached for her hands as Eric shuffled over. Miriam squeezed her hands as tears filled her eyes.

"Mom…" Deanna sucked in a shaky breath. "It's really you."

Tears streamed down her mother's face. "Yes, baby. It's me."

Deanna began to sob. This moment was twenty-three years in the making, and she was overwhelmed.

Eric stood up, and Miriam quickly took the spot that he had vacated so she could sit beside her daughter. "I saw you on the news," she said. "I saw what my father did to you. And I knew then that I had to come. I had to come back to you."

"So he really *is* my…" Deanna couldn't say anything more, her throat was too clogged with emotion. But as her mother placed her hand on her cheek, Deanna turned her face inward, allowing her mother's hand to fully caress her face.

If this moment were a dream, she never wanted to wake up.

"I'm so sorry, baby. I should have told you, all of you, the truth a long time ago. Because I didn't, I put you in harm's way. It's just that I thought I could deal with it on my own, take care of the situation. Once Jean died, I went back to Georgia. I was determined to find proof of my mother's murder. I knew that was the only way to take my father down so

I could finally be safe. So we all could be safe. But the police only considered her a missing person—based on a report my father filed twenty-four years ago. I couldn't find any proof that he killed her."

Her mother had said a lot, too much information to digest at this moment. And all that mattered to Deanna right now was that the moment she and her sisters had waited for had finally arrived.

"You're here," Deanna said. "You're really here."

"I know, baby. I'm here."

Suddenly, Callie and Natalie were at the bed, both of them placing a hand on their mother's shoulders. Her sisters were crying. This moment was overwhelming for all of them.

"I should have known he was lying," Deanna said, now addressing some of what her grandfather had said about her mother. "He said the most awful things about you. He told me you were a killer. And…and he sounded so truthful. It made me doubt you, and I'm so sorry for that. So many years I've wanted to find you, and he came, and he fed me lies…"

"Hush," her mother cooed. "I'm the one who should have told you the truth years ago. Calvin is nothing if not a skilled liar. It's part of what makes him so dangerous. Please don't blame yourself. I blame myself, because I know that if I had told you the truth you never would have met him. The fact that he almost killed you…" Miriam's eyes misted again. And when she spoke once more, her voice was thick with her tears. "I would never forgive myself if something happened to you."

"What happened?" Deanna asked her. "What happened that night, in Georgia?"

"I'll tell you," Miriam said. "I'll tell you everything."

Suddenly, there was a loud banging sound, like a door slamming against the wall. Deanna's eyes flew forward, toward the front door.

And just before she heard her sisters scream, her entire body froze.

Because Calvin Harrison had just charged into the house with a gun.

Eric had been standing near the door when he heard it slam open. Immediately, his eyes had gone from Deanna and her mother to the door, a sense of panic instantly gripping him. And what he saw confirmed that he had reason to be panicked.

It was Calvin. He was certain that it was the man based on the photo of him that had been on the news. And even more certain when the gray-haired man whipped a gun from his jacket pocket.

Calvin leveled his eyes on his daughter. "This is your day of reckoning, Mary."

A surge of adrenaline rushed through Eric's veins. He didn't know if Nigel had his gun or not, but he had gone upstairs and there was no time to wait for him to come back either way.

Eric didn't think. He acted. Acted to protect Deanna and her family without regard for his own safety.

"Drop the gun, Calvin," he said, taking a step toward him.

"Stand back," Calvin warned. "This is between me and Mary."

Eric didn't stop, and Calvin pointed the gun at him.

And then Eric lunged forward. He heard the screams a moment before the shot went off in the room.

Deanna watched everything in horror. Eric being the hero, charging at Calvin. Calvin pointing the gun at him. Eric jumping onto Calvin, knocking the older man onto his back.

The gun going off.

The next moments passed in slow motion, as Deanna

watched for movement from Eric. She could hear her heart pounding, mixing with the sound of her screams.

At last, Eric moved. He gripped the wrist of Calvin's hand holding the gun and banged it on the hardwood floor until the gun went flying from Calvin's hand. It was then that Deanna noticed there was a hole in the wall above where Uncle Dave was previously before he jumped at the sound of the gunshot. Dear God in heaven, her uncle had come close to getting shot.

Nigel charged down from upstairs and joined the melee, helping to restrain Calvin. He and Eric wrestled the man until he was turned over on his stomach.

"Eric!" Deanna exclaimed. "Are you okay?"

"I'm fine," Eric told her.

Deanna saw blood on his cheek, and her stomach tightened with fear. "No, Eric—you are not okay." She hurried toward him. "You're bleeding."

"I wasn't shot."

"But you could have been." She touched his face, brushing the blood away, and saw that he'd only suffered a small gash as a result of the struggle. "Eric, that was foolish." Deanna framed his cheek. "But so incredibly brave."

"I called the police," Callie announced. She drew Kwame into an embrace and looked as though she didn't want to let him go.

"It's over," Miriam said, and she wrapped her arms tightly around Deanna. "It's over. Thank God!"

The drama ended as quickly as it had begun. Although in all reality, this was a night twenty-four years in the making.

The police came and carted Calvin off to jail, where the charges against him would include attempted murder as well as the twenty-four-year-old murder of his wife.

Miriam sat on the sofa bed now, surrounded by her children. The excitement had calmed down, and the crying had come to an end. She said to them, "I can tell you everything now."

Deanna gripped her hand. Everyone was sitting as close to her as possible, surrounding her with their love and presence.

"I believe he came for you specifically," Miriam said, facing Deanna. "That's why he reached out to you in particular. Because he knew that you were the one who had witnessed what happened that night."

Deanna nodded jerkily. Everything that had transpired, as well as the story Calvin had told her, had led to the pieces of the puzzle coming together in her mind.

No wonder she had never seen her and Brian's faces in her frequent nightmares. Because the nightmares were about a repressed memory of a traumatic event from her childhood.

It had been her grandparents she had seen struggling in her dream. And then her grandfather had struck her grandmother with a gun, knocking her to the ground before shooting her.

"He knows there's no statute of limitations on murder," Miriam went on. "He must have been afraid that one day you would remember what had happened. And as long as you were a possible witness to his crime, you could take him down. He also knew that I was a threat, which is why I ran, why I changed my name. And I'm so glad I did, because with a different surname and you and Natalie getting some national attention, he didn't put it together that you were my children. I'm so sorry I left you all, but your grandfather was a very dangerous man." Miriam lowered her eyes, as if ashamed. "And I made bad choices. I guess I followed what I knew. I dated men who were abusive, like my father. Men who were on the wrong side of the law. Jean, God bless her soul, was able to find a good man, and she never let him go. Me...my whole life has been a big mess."

Miriam began to cry again, this time out of shame.

Deanna put her arms around her mother and held her

tightly. "We never stopped loving you," she said. "We never judged you, even when Auntie Jean told us that you left because you'd gotten involved with shady characters."

"If nothing else," Natalie chimed in, "we loved you more. We loved you more because we knew that you had sacrificed everything to protect us. You shouldn't have had to live your life without your children. And yet you did. You gave us up—the hardest thing for a mother to do—to make sure that no harm ever came to us."

"Exactly," Callie said, and Deanna knew that for her sister to say these words truly offered healing for their mother, for all of them. "In the beginning, I didn't understand why you didn't come back. I thought you'd abandoned us. There's no doubt that we all felt that, at least at some point. But like Natalie said, leaving your children has got to be the hardest thing in the world. As a mother, I know that."

"I missed out on so much," Miriam said. "Getting to know my grandson all these years."

"Because you left to protect us," Callie stressed. "And that's all that matters. The love we had never died. I may have questioned it, but that doesn't matter now. None of that matters now." Tears began to fall from Callie's eyes. "What matters is that you're here, Mom. And we couldn't be happier."

The tears fell freely now, all of the women crying happy tears. God had allowed them to reunite. Anything could have happened to them during these twenty-three years, and yet they were all here now, alive and well and able to enjoy this most splendid of reunions.

"You all… I never stopped thinking about you. Not a day in my life went by that I didn't think about you." Miriam looked at them in turn.

"We know," Natalie said, and she squeezed her mother's hand. "I could feel the love, Mom. I could feel it, even though we weren't together."

"And now there's nothing keeping us from each other." Deanna brushed her tears. "We can finally be a family again."

"I just wish I never gave you girls up," Miriam said. "I wish I had stayed and fought. I wish I had tried."

Deanna said, "Mom, forgive yourself for that. Because we forgive you. You left us with your sister, someone you trusted implicitly. You did that to protect us. And you gave us a good life. We had a good life with Auntie Jean and Uncle Dave." Deanna's voice cracked a little, but then she went on. "And more than that, because you brought us here, and because we had to come back here for Auntie Jean's funeral, it allowed us to find love. Nigel and Callie were meant to be from the moment they started to date. Natalie has found someone she's going to spend forever with. And me..." She looked up at Eric. "You've met the man I love."

"The hero of the hour," Miriam said, looking in his direction and smiling.

"Everything you sacrificed for us has led to good," Deanna went on. "We're happy. And now you being back has made us all complete."

Miriam's eyes glistened with tears as she listened to the words Deanna said. And then she put her arms around Deanna and Natalie and leaned forward so that her face was pressing against Callie's forehead.

"I guess I did do something right," she said softly. "Because somehow, my three beautiful girls grew up to be three beautiful, fantastic, caring women."

"Our family is back together again," Natalie said, not bothering to wipe her happy tears.

"And speaking of family," Eric began as he stepped forward now from where he'd been sitting on the staircase, after having allowed the mother and daughters to have some time. "I want to ask Deanna to marry me. You're all here. I think it's appropriate now. I love her. This—what happened today and what happened with Calvin—has made it all too clear that I don't want to spend another moment without her."

Deanna looked up at Eric in shock. "You want to marry me?"

"I want nothing more," Eric told her. He bent onto his haunches in front of her and took her face in his hands. "I love you, baby. More than anything in the world. And I want you to be my wife."

And then his lips met hers, soft and sweet and full of promise.

"Well," Miriam said when they pulled apart. "Are you going to give the man an answer?"

"Yes!" Deanna exclaimed with a giggle. "Yes, Eric—I'll definitely marry you!"

Epilogue

Three months later...

As winter weddings went, this one was magical. The bride wore a full-length white dress with a wide skirt and a fitted bodice and completed the winter gown with a faux-fur shawl. Her veil was adorned with Austrian crystals. But even behind the veil, her tears were still evident.

Happy tears. Because this was a moment she had waited so long for.

There was a fresh dusting of snow outside, adding to the picturesque magic of the day.

Callie gazed out the window of the bridal suite. "I can't believe this moment is here."

"It's here," Natalie said, a smile brightening her face. "Believe it."

Deanna fussed with Callie's veil, making sure it was just right. "You look stunning, sis. Absolutely beautiful in this winter gown. And the white patent-leather boots…the perfect touch."

"I got so used to the warmth in Florida," Callie said, "I can't believe I'm getting married in January."

"Because you and Nigel waited long enough to be together," Natalie told her. "This is perfect, Callie. A perfect day. And you are the most beautiful bride ever. Seriously."

"You two." Grinning, Callie took Natalie's hand in one of hers and Deanna's in the other. "I love both of you so much."

"And we love you back," Deanna said, reaching for Natalie's free hand. Now they all stood holding hands, forming a circle.

"Isn't it amazing?" Callie went on. "Now that we're back here, everything is falling into place in our lives. It's like once we stopped running and returned home, we got everything we ever wanted."

"You're going to make me cry," Natalie said.

"Me, too," Deanna chimed. She didn't want her makeup to be ruined.

"I'm about to marry the man of my dreams," Callie continued. "But I wanted you both to know that the love I feel for you could not be greater. No matter where we go from here, if we live in different cities, different states, we'll always be in touch. Never again will our bond of sisterhood be broken. The same way the three of us stand here holding hands, this is how we'll be from now on. United."

"Oh, there you go," Natalie said, and tears spilled down her face. She had to wipe at them, which she did delicately so as not to ruin the makeup that had taken two hours to perfect.

"I love you, Natalie." Callie then faced Deanna. "And I love you, too, Deanna."

"I love you, too," Deanna said.

"And I love you," Natalie said.

They repeated words of love to each other and then came together in a group hug.

Once they pulled apart, Deanna said, "Nigel's waiting." She grinned from ear to ear. "He's been waiting for ten years. Go get your man."

The wedding had been a true winter wonderland experience. From the ice sculpture in the middle of the reception hall, to the strings of crystals hanging from the ceiling, to the snowflake patterns of lights dancing over the dimmed room, everything about this spoke of a winter dreamland.

Callie, finally tired of the white leather boots she had worn, had shucked them. Now she was barefoot as she danced the first dance with her new husband.

Danced while Deanna sang one of her love songs.

Deanna gazed at Callie with happiness and love in her heart as she crooned about finding a love that stood the test of time. And when the song came to an end, Callie and Nigel shared a kiss, which made everyone cheer wildly. It was clear to everyone that the bride and groom were truly in love.

Pulling apart from Nigel, Callie rushed over to Deanna and hugged her long and hard. "That was beautiful, sis," she said, her voice full of emotion. "Thank you so much."

"For this next song, I need the Hart sisters on the dance floor," the DJ announced. "Callie, Deanna and Natalie, please come to the dance floor."

Deanna's eyes narrowed in confusion, but Callie beamed as she took her hand. As Callie led her onto the dance floor, they saw Natalie walking onto it from the other side. She looked as confused as Deanna felt.

And then music began to play. It didn't take long for Deanna to recognize the opening sequence to Chubb Rock's "Treat 'Em Right."

"Oh, my God," Deanna said, the significance of this song hitting her instantly. "You're kidding me."

"So you remember," Callie said.

"How could I forget?" Deanna asked.

Natalie was already shaking her body to the song that had been the sisters' favorite when they were young. Whenever they'd been upset as children, they put this song on and danced their problems away.

Callie was the next to start to get down. Then, shamelessly, Deanna began to boogie—and she really let loose when the chorus began.

Soon, the roomful of guests was surrounding them. They clapped and cheered the sisters on as they danced as though they didn't have a care in the world.

And the crowd really went wild when their mother joined them on the floor for the last part of the song and got down with her daughters.

As the song came to a close, Callie pulled her sisters and mother close and they shared a group hug. All the years they had been apart had slipped away, and the only thing that mattered was now, and what tomorrow would bring.

"I love you girls so much," Miriam said. "We'll never be apart again. Not ever."

And when they pulled apart, all of their eyes were filled with tears. Their mother's words resonated with Deanna. No matter where they would go from this point on, they would always be together in their hearts. Never would they let anything come between them again.

After all, they had gone through the worst trials and tribulations that any family could go through and they had survived. And now, they were closer than ever.

A love song began, and Nigel quickly found his bride. He slipped an arm around her waist, and Callie turned to face him, smiling up at her man.

As Deanna gazed at them with affection, she felt hands close around her own waist. Then she turned and looked into the face of the man she loved.

"Can I have this dance?" Eric asked.

"Of course you can have this dance."

Laying her head on his shoulder, Deanna couldn't help thinking how her life had changed so much in the last months. She was happy—really and truly happy—for the first time in forever.

For now, Eric was keeping his job in Cleveland. He didn't want to move and force Deanna to have to part from her newly reunited family. She was his first priority, and she adored him for that.

Deanna looked up at him and tenderly stroked his face. She couldn't help thinking that she was the luckiest woman alive. Whether God blessed them with children or not, she knew her life with him would be complete.

"What are you thinking?" Eric asked her.

"That I'm happy," Deanna said. "So happy."

"I know, baby. Me, too."

Deanna extended her left hand as they swayed together so that she could gaze at the stunning engagement ring Eric had given her a week after the drama had unfolded at her uncle's house. Her big day was coming in the summer. And Natalie and Michael were getting married before that, in April.

Deanna couldn't wait to share this magical moment of wedding day bliss with her husband.

But until then, this would do.

It would do just fine.

* * * * *

REQUEST YOUR FREE BOOKS!

2 FREE NOVELS
PLUS 2 **FREE GIFTS!**

KIMANI
ROMANCE

Love's ultimate destination!

An appetite for seduction...